All Quiet in Mindanao

A novel of corruption

Elizabeth Gowans

Chapter One

Efigenia left the car at the foot of the hill. She had made the rule that all coming to the Shrine should climb on foot for this gave the sense of *ascent* from everyday life and the shrines she had visited in Europe had all involved climbs from crowded coach parks, past souvenir stands cluttered with nuns. Six in the morning. Most of her husband's workers would be out in the plantation now, spraying fungicides, nematicides. No protective masks of course. They coughed quietly. In the shrine she would pray that Victor would take better care of these details. That life had cast her in a different lot from the workers who arose at four and hastily breakfasted on cold rice saved from the previous night, did not trouble her. If she awakened early enough she could imagine them stepping barefoot into the darkness, the hardened soles of their feet crushing foliage as they cut towards the dirt road to fall in silently with others of their kind. She paused to rest. Victor had given her this section of land for her shrine to the Infant of Prague, the statue she had brought back. He had done this to keep her happy: had loaned a foreman, workers to clear the old coconut trees and grass it over. But the grass could not be sat on. It was itchy. The foreman had suggested leaving in the stumps of the coconut palms for visitors to sit on but she had installed cement benches in keeping with the dignity of the place and lain the old coconut trees in the parking lot at the foot of the hill. Few came by car however. The sort who came used the public bus and ignored the cement benches. It was because she was overweight, the result of dutiful childbearing, that she found the humidity exhausting. Dutiful childbearing *and* the obligation as wife of one of

3

the richest men in Mindanao, to host social dinners and gatherings.

At the side of the hill there was movement in the two shacks she had permitted to be erected, the one to sell candles and medals, the other ready-made clothes and necklaces for the statue. Victor did not appreciate it but *she* understood the meaning that clothing the statue held out to those in rags. In the Cathedral – built largely with Victor's money – they whispered fears to statues, kissed, touched their feet, promised. *Her* statue had a wardrobe worth several thousand pesos already. Though none had heard of the Infant of Prague, the fact that it had been the Señora who had brought the statue, that it had come from Europe, that she said it had a history of miracles had been sufficient for them to welcome it like the next addition to their ever-expanding families.

Stepping into the darkness of the shrine she knelt. There had been no miracle yet but one day there would be. Perhaps a spring would well up and cures would take place. It took faith. She pulled the dead flowers from the jars, tossed them into a bin, picked up a dropped match from the votive rack and hesitated. If she lit the remainder of the candles it would make the place more cheerful but perhaps the statue would prefer to save the candles for when people came. She stared at its outstretched arms. When she and Victor had visited Prague, conscious of being non-European, the sight of the Infant stretching out its arms had been overwhelming. Even now as it waited to be dressed she felt moved, not as a mother towards a child but as a person running to Love. She would change Victor. She would see he was better to the workers and built them a proper hospital and sports facilities.

At that moment in Davao City, Father Torres was locking the door of the Cathedral Victor had largely built though, as the Bishop had said, they had to balance the provenance of the money with the advantages of *having* a Cathedral in such an outpost. To Father Torres' mind, they would have been better off saying Mass in the open than accepting that man's money, a man for whom building the Cathedral had been a master coup. How could he, Father Torres, suggest to the labourers who stood cap in hand, that the patron they prayed for, the man whose soul they begged God would judge kindly for giving them this modern Cathedral, the only shaded place with glass windows most of them ever entered – was the utter negation of all the Our Father stood for? Descending the steps he locked eyes with the papaya seller, noticing the man's eyes fill with tears, no doubt because it was their priest's last day, because he and his entire order were being booted out, sent packing to the States for 'political interference'. In point of fact, he thought, turning to look back at the modern door he hated, he should have made his last Mass a political gesture.   Instead of raising the Eucharist and saying: "This is my body which will be given up for you" – he should have lifted up a banana, because it was the banana and the wealth it represented that had sown greed in the hearts of men like Victor Salcedo and taken the lives of the poor.

He crossed the road. Twenty years in the Philippines was a long time. He would return to the United States, what? An aged Mexican-American priest, shunted off as chaplain to some migrant group of Californian lettuce pickers? And in his place would come – *was already coming* – an Englishman. Such artifice! The English, who served Africa and countries unlike the Philippines where they had historical ties! This, the Bishop had said, was the Americans' fault for interfering. Having no connection with the Philippines and knowing nothing about it, the new priest could simply say Mass and mind his own business. So be it. Or should he tell this English priest that despite the packed churches, Christianity was irrelevant to the life practiced in this so called Catholic country? That it was no more than a sloppy old coat painted on by the Spaniards that none had bothered to chip off! Could he go one better and say that underneath the mask of democracy the Americans thought had 'taken', couched the real system, *raw power?* They may have fooled the Spaniards for four hundred years, these Filipinos; may have taken in the Americans for half a century but what had gotten through? The "Patron" idea from the Spanish and democracy – meaning mob rule – from the Americans. The Christianity his church had brought had justified the idea of authority and paved the way for men like Victor Salcedo to prey on others while emasculating those he had wronged 'til they couldn't retaliate. Underneath their easy use of the English language, like that ridiculous woman with her ridiculous shrine, these were a pre-Christian people bargaining with Fate and interpreting the Will of God as some form of arbitrary sadism. Oh yes it was time to go! He felt the papaya seller watching him cross the road, ready to busy himself rearranging his crescent shaped papaya slices should he turn round. People didn't want to talk to him anymore. The slatted branches of the coconut trees began to clatter in the wind – a sign rain would start.

Out at the airport, Victor Salcedo prepared to meet the new priest. He strutted, beaming at people behind cordons. After the welcome committee, consisting of speeches and a little girl to give flowers – the English liked flowers – the new priest would be taken in one of Salcedo's own S.D.C.I (Salcedo Development Company Inc.) white Chevrolet 2-door pickups to the town and through it, passing the new Cathedral *twice.* He would lean forward, pointing out the main centre, the Bank, the newspaper office, the 'bad' end of town - concerned face – explaining he was revitalizing it: indicating his banana trucks backing, filling up. They would pass the warehouses, now no longer needed he would explain as a refrigeration plant and generator had been installed at the plantation. He might say they were going to be used for what? Something communal. Further up the road the priest would see labourers scrambling onto pickups, handing plastic bowls up through bus windows – purchases made, he would point out, with money he had paid them. They would bump across the wide river with its scattering of huts on stilts (people who did *not* work for him), their few rags drying on sticks. There would be a smell. The priest would probably fan himself as the road rose passing *his wife's shrine to the Infant of Prague* on the right – then climb through the fallen coconut trees of the old Spanish plantation 'til it reached and turned in at the gates of Mansion Salcedo. Always charming, his wife would greet them: his elder sons Ricky and Fredo, would accompany him to wash up before drinks on the back balcony with its view of the sea, then lunch in the dining room, the entire family – all eight children - being present. A good Catholic family! He would invite the priest to say Grace. In the afternoon they would do a tour

7

of the plantation, he earnestly pointing out the benefits *he had provided* for the workers, the barracks they could sleep in so they did not have to travel from town, the basketball pitch, the shop where they could buy tinned mackerel, cooking oil and rice. In the evening Efigenia could talk to him about the women's classes in childcare and embroidery. How old would this priest be? Could he be silver haired, easy to call 'father'? Or a young man the matrons would take joy in.

Fr. Jack rested his head on the plane window watching the small shadow of the plane crossing a giant pineapple plantation, denuded hills scored with pineapple tops like patterned paper.

"Doesn't anyone live there?" he asked the woman next to him.

She waved her fan.

"Gone away?" he asked.

"Gone away," she nodded.

He wiped his neck. His trousers were tight. Last time the BAC–one eleven had put down all the cool air had left the cabin and flies buzzed in. People around him slept with their mouths open.

Victor Salcedo shifted from foot to foot. The flight was late. The plane had been down five minutes already and no one that looked like a priest had got off. It would be awkward if this priest turned out to be the kind who missed planes or made unlikely acquaintances.

Gradually the airport emptied. The plane taxied. Victor strutted to Information.

"What time does the next flight from Manila arrive?"

"18.30 Mr. Salcedo, Sir."

"I have the booking details of a particular passenger. I gave strict instructions to be notified should he fail to board the aircraft." Victor glared at the young woman.

"The flight has departed. Where is he?"

"May I have the passenger's name?"

"Fr. Jack Mountjoy."

"A Jack Mountjoy was on that flight. He alighted at Cagayon de Oro."

"In the name of God!"

"It may have been a mistake - "

"For your sake, let us hope it wasn't."

Jack pulled himself up onto the bus, easing his way between people and bundles. Unfamiliar pop came from the bus radio. The driver, stretching and scratching, was easing himself into the right state of mind to drive 200 kms to Davao City, glancing lazily back down the bus at the banana peels, biscuit wrappers falling into the gangway. He switched on, the bus throbbing to the gear box's rattle.

"Where do we stop first?" Jack raised his voice at his elderly neighbour. "We stop 3 times?"

The man smiled, called something to the driver who turned around, shouting over the engine's roar: "You want toilet Mister?"

"I'm OK– " Jack waved thanks, smiled at his neighbour. He'd wanted to see if where they'd stop would have a church so he could walk in, get a feel for the place: do it alone rather than be introduced to a building, told where the lights switched on. He began to doze. The bus was stuffy. It drove on through hills, bends, the dense green unknowable heart of Mindanao…

Emerging as from a sleep, the bus swung a noisy U round a plaza and screeched to a halt, splitting open like an overripe pomegranate to disgorge sticky passengers who bunched around food stands, wandered looking for latrines.

Jack sat. There - across the dusty space – was a church. Here was the private experience he wanted which would tell him if he'd done the right thing in coming to this country. He stepped carefully from the bus. Everything was important. The manner in which he entered the building was important. He glanced around. Apart from an old dog lolling in the church entrance for shade, no one was watching. He stepped in.

With minute care his eyes took in a large dead leaf halfway up the aisle. He walked towards it, his left hand moving across the names of donors painted in uneven letters on pews. The air was musty. To one side a brightly hued Archangel wearing knitted cap and tennis skirt, waved a *bolo* threateningly towards a line of ants crawling from a rotted pew. Ahead the altar was guarded by two statues, a St. Anthony and a St. Joseph, different sizes, probably handed down. Each held a Child Jesus and a long-stemmed lily, their gaze seeming to fall behind him on the mange ridden bitch who'd followed him into the church and stood on three legs, her scratching tearing the silence.

In an alcove, a statue of Our Lady stood on a crate against a painted scene of rice fields and fishing huts, a hand extended in blessing over paper flowers in dried milk tins and rum bottles which waved cheerily at her feet …. Beside her was a rickety confessional, with a yellow plastic shower curtain.

He stood quite still.

At that moment, in a farmhouse made of planking deep in the green denseness 80 miles away, a family of settlers were beginning their evening meal, giving thanks to God for the land they had cleared, for their hopes and dreams, for the earth that sustained them.

Forty-six-year-old mother Emerenciana bowed her head to say Grace. Thank you God for the food we eat which we have grown with our hands; for my husband, Rustico, our healthy children and grandchildren. Husband Rustico, fifty-five years old, prayed that before he was truly old his children would be secure. He glanced at oldest son Romeo's wife Rosing, reaching back the hands of her children as they stretched across the table, raising her own eyes to her brother-in-law Rodolfo. Twenty-four and married but still only the one child. 'Lord grant him more!' she prayed. "I have five already!" Head bowed, opposite her, Robencio prayed for himself. "How will I meet a young woman, Lord, with no trips to town? I am twenty-one and You know it. We can go to town regularly if we have surplus to market..." At the table's end, fourteen-year-old Adan thanked God for the family that had taken him in. "Please Father. We must not be the only family here. Send others". He looked earnestly at the Sacred Heart picture on the wall and the palm cross above the door. "Wilma is thirteen and Violeta eleven. They are growing up. Oscar is ten Father and Edgar seven though he sucks his thumb. Let people come and clear land near us so we will not be alone. Baby Cresmalin too. Give her a friend!"

"Begin!" Emerenciana announced.

They stretched for the food, their shadows flickering on the walls, the sound of their conversation a warm buzz. Rustico leaned forward, pumping the lamp as night chased day without that gentle dusk they'd known on the coast. But the forest was servant and shield. He sat back down. Suddenly their dog growled, then burst into panicked barks. A shot rang out. Hands holding forks froze, mouths gaped.

"Waray lumusad!" (No one may leave!) a voice outside shouted. Even as adults pushed the children under the table, automatic gunfire tore through the walls, sending enamel plates flying. As the oil lamp smashed Oscar glimpsed his grandfather across the room, reaching for his rifle, clutching his chest.

"Pappa!" He began to crawl.

"Come back!" Robencio pulled at him, half standing, catching a bullet in his thigh, buckling over, the bullet veering into his stomach. Oscar cringed. Uncle's head was splitting open, the room ringing with shots.

"Here!" Emerenciana, pulled Oscar under the table but as she pulled him, bullets sliced his spine, his entrails spattering his siblings. There was silence but for frightened breathing in the pitch-black room. Then a mad scramble to get out.

"Stay!" Emerenciana urged.
They ran into a wall of shots.

Stifling his breath under a bush, Edgar heard his father pleading: "Sir! *Ayaw kami pagblati kay warayy man kami sala!"* (Sir! Please don't do anything to us! We have done nothing wrong!") He could see him pinned to the ground by a rifle held by a soldier. Crack! The soldier let go the fire into his father's stomach. Romeo's body spun.

Edgar cried out. Hearing it, a soldier lifted a branch with his rifle nose, locked eyes with the frightened child.

"Ayaw kay bata iton!" he muttered, letting the branch drop.

Clutching the remains of her thumb, Wilma heard the soldiers cross the verandah, enter the room where they'd been eating. She could now see them with their flashlights emptying tins, stuffing cash, ball pens in their pockets, scattering clothes. A soldier bent to grasp a sack of rice between his thighs, lift it to his shoulders.

By the time light came up, the soldiers were long gone. Face swollen with grief, Emerenciana groped in the ransacked cupboard, bloodied hands shaking the empty money tin. Behind her, both her husband and her second oldest son were stiffening on the floor. Under the table, in pieces, little Oscar. Beyond the window, her remaining grown sons, their wives lay blood spattered, curled. She wiped the heel of her dirty hand over her face. Adan. Where was he? From the bushes, Wilma watched her grandmother moving about, blood soaked dress stuck to her thighs, calling. Holding baby Cresmalin, Violeta stood to the side of the broken building. In shock, Edgar did not call out or uncurl from under the bush. He was not found.

Taking Wilma, Violeta and baby Cresmalin, Emerenciana walked through their banana plants, sugar cane and *camote*, their coffee bushes, their patch of corn. The only sound came from a disturbed parakeet and a cicada. By noon they had reached the nearest small town. Emerenciana left the children in the church and made for the police station. Then hesitated. But entered. The wall was painted green. There was a large picture of President Ferdinand Marcos on the wall, looking grand, his hand across his chest. At a plain table in front of the picture sat a young policeman, a shining INP (Integrated National Police) badge on his chest, his fawn uniform frighteningly clean. He stared at Emerenciana and said nothing. As she spoke he said nothing. Her voice rose and rose in the bare room. Finally he shook his head.

"They were soldiers! They were in uniform!"

He reached a pack of imported filter cigarettes from his chest pocket.

"What was their regiment?"

"Their what?"

He took one cigarette out, tapped it on the table.

"Their constabulary."

Emerenciana stood mutely.

He put the cigarettes back in his shirt pocket.

"You are trying to make trouble. There are no battalions in this area. I'd better take your details -"

She stepped back.

In the bright sun, Emerenciana retraced her steps down the dusty street, its crumbling stores, hoardings for San Miguel beer, for Extra Smooth Quality Gin telling her to be gone.... A man grading peanuts by the petrol pump looked up as she passed.

"Where did you break your journey?" Victor asked pleasantly. "You must have arrived yesterday."

"I don't recall the town's name. Just somewhere I got off the bus -"

"You crossed Mindanao by bus? A local bus?" Efigenia gasped. Jack looked questioning.

"I admire that," she added. "People were - friendly towards you?"

"Very - "

Efigenia lifted a pitcher from a table laden with glass and silver. "Fresh lime with papaya," she beamed.

"The English say *pawpaw*," Victor corrected. "Would you prefer a beer?"

"This is fine. We say *papaya* too."

"You will find it very quiet here Father," Victor said moving towards the window. "Mindanao is a sleepy place." He turned to look at Jack. "You must regard our home as your home."

In the heat which magnified sounds, Jack heard a tinkle below, a door opening in the far reaches of their house, an argument beginning, a woman's voice rising higher and higher.

"Imagine you spending a night in a local hotel without knowing anyone!" Efigenia said quickly.

"I'm sorry I caused you worry. I didn't know I was expected. By you."

"Excuse me." Victor strode from the room.

"My husband's position as a plantation owner means that occasionally workers have problems. They come to us." Efigenia stood awkwardly. "But Victor is wonderful."

Jack crossed to the window.

"Coming from different islands, as they do, they disagree," she continued lamely. "It's to be expected. The Philippines is like a plate dropped from Heaven to smash in a thousand pieces on the sea."

Jack peered down. "I did see a lot of islands."

"They have all come for the opportunities of course," Efigenia continued, wishing him far from the window. "I admire that. Come sit down." Jack stared from the window. "Leave it to Victor, Father – "

She joined him at the window.

A shouting woman in bloodstained dress was backing from the house.

"Poor soul" she gasped. "What can have happened?"

"There's a child watching —"

"Oh do be careful Victor!" Efigenia cried. "He's walking towards her! It could be a trick!" The woman flung herself on her knees in front of Victor who crouched, wobbling on his haunches, shirt tight across his stomach, one hand on the woman's elbow, trying to help her up.

"Women like that —(!)"

"What's she saying?"

Suddenly the woman burst into angry speech, gesturing men shooting wantonly. Victor was nodding.

Efigenia shook her head.

Victor again tried to raise her to her feet. She clearly disagreed, pulling, arguing. He became firm.

"I'm sorry you had to see this," Efigenia fumbled, pulling at Jack's elbow. "It can happen for money. For all we know it's animal blood."

"*Women like that*, you said. What about *women like that?*"

"What do they know of politics? It breaks Victor's heart."

"Politics?"

"Communists in the hills cause a lot of trouble. They make poor people support them." She nodded nervously at a maid who had come in to place a shellfish salad on the table. Jack looked from the window. The woman was slinking away. Victor, the knees of his pants besmirched, head glistening, was entering the house.

Around them the plantation stretched in hectare upon green silent hectare.

Another maid entered with a rice dish, followed eventually by Victor in a clean shirt.

"Sorry to keep you waiting. I do apologise." He moved to the head of the table. "Will you say Grace?" Jack passed him, heading for the door. "Where are you going?"

"To see what I can do for that woman – "

"It was *me* she came to."

"As a priest – my duty to the people here – "

"Is to say Mass and hear confessions," Victor said, indicating the spread table, steering him firmly back. "Anything else you need not concern yourself with."

Chapter 2

Jack awakened next morning to the sound of a pitcher being placed gently by his head.

"It's a privilege to have a priest staying – " Efigenia whispered, tiptoeing from the room.

"Thank you. I -"

She stopped in the doorway. "You want to leave! There's nowhere for you! That building on the airport road - you didn't see it because you came by bus - That's where the American Missionary Fathers … But - um - Our – we call them *native clergy* – live in a decayed –"

"I don't mind what con – "

"You don't speak *Tagalog,* Father. You *must* stay here."

"Please call me Ja- "

"Did Victor offend you - when he said you should just say Mass and hear confessions? He only meant -"

"Of course not."

She looked earnestly at Jack as if not used herself to being taken seriously. "He's renovating the Cathedral rooms so you can be attached to it now. Please allow him a few more days. We requested a foreign priest because religions have a way of - of - *hybridizing* left to themselves. We -"

"But you have clergy - "

"I've been to Rome. I know what a backwater we are. Especially Mindanao. Yes, people come here from Luzon, Cebu, Samar thinking there is a pot of gold waiting. You can find antique fire screens here but not a piece of Formica. It's... I mean we have very little -"

A massive VROOOMM cut off her speech. "My daughter Norma," Efigenia apologised, glancing from the window at a white convertible, tires spitting gravel, streaking towards the road.

"Breakfast is ready when you are."

A small maid, little more than a child, waited on Jack at breakfast.

"Is there a bus into town?"

She smiled angelically.

"Bus?" He made steering wheel signs. "Davao?"

"Davao?" she repeated, big eyed.

An older maid joined her.

"No bus. Car. You wait."

"When? Car?"

"Sun-day."

"Car. Sunday? Davao?"

"Church!"

Efigenia bustled in. "Are the girls looking after you? Loretta has started English. Children, Father is our new priest." She said slowly in English, repeating herself in Tagalog. "If you have no other plan, after lunch Ricky and Fredo will show you around."

Norma slowed in the morning traffic, the roar of an old Pantranco bus smothering her stereo as its driver wrenched the gears from third to first, pulled on the handbrake, in an effort to stop for an ox cart laden with copra. Waiting in its fumes, Norma checked her mirror. He was still following her. Leaning around the bus she saw a wheel had come off the ox cart, which had lurched sending sacks of copra bouncing into the road. The sacks had split, copra rolling under vehicles and onto pavements where annoyed shop owners, trying to swill their shop fronts, were kicking it back into the road. The peasant was running barefoot through traffic, bending to reach under vehicles to retrieve his precious crop. She clicked her tongue impatiently. A nearby record shop came loudly to life.

Norma drove to the University. He was still following. Students with books and bags chattered in groups, trying to catch each other's eyes. She stopped, got out by the NO DRUG –TAKING, NO HAZING ON CAMPUS, NO DRINKING OR POLITICAL MEETINGS signboard and pretended to read a timetable change notice then got back in the car, drove through the University and out the other side. He had not even bothered following her round the last corners! She pulled up outside a two-storey house with iron railings and a locked gate, she waited. If he was watching, he would report that she had gone round to her boyfriend's. She got out, rang the bell, swept past the maid as the front door opened and went upstairs. A few moments later an upstairs window was thrown up and she and the young man leaned out, giggling to each other then withdrew, half shutting the window but letting American mood music waft out.

Inside the room the young man got on with the essay he was writing. Behind him Norma pulled off her jeans, drew an old skirt from a cupboard, loosed her hair, closed the door quietly and passed through the kitchen unnoticed by the maid picking rice grains from a pan, flicking them through the barred window. Stepping from the back entrance she ran after a PU (public utility) and squeezed into it. PUs were handy in that it was impossible to recognise anyone, stuffed together with heads bent, stopping at the least chance of a fare, agreeing to pass every which way, baskets being handed up and down...... Norma looked at her watch then worked through the day's plan. *Could* she jump out at the market place and cut along the main street? Too risky.

Reaching the Cathedral at five past ten she ambled up the steps in a lackadaisical way, knowing the papaya seller would take her to be a local girl making a novena for a special intention...... He did not look up.

After the bright sunlight, the Cathedral was dark inside. Specks of light, candles flickered in its depths. She passed the daily Mass goers spotting the pews, genuflected and entered the pew she or her replacement used, straight in the native priest's line of vision, seeing him notice her. Behind and around, lulled by the sleepy rhythm of prayer, the congregation noticed nothing. Alert, Norma awaited the Consecration.

"Lord, I am not worthy –"

At the precise moment when the priest raised the host and all heads in the church were bowed, hers was erect, staring. Almost imperceptibly the priest moved his eyes from side to side, shaking his head at her. The first woman went to communion, then the second, followed by the simpleton from the back who was at every Mass. Norma dipped her head while they passed. The sacristan would be there. He'd know her. The priest finished serving communion, replaced the chalice in the tabernacle and brought the Mass to a close.

Head bowed, like those around her, Norma crossed herself, waited while women got to their feet, shuffled off to light candles, kiss statues. She walked to the back of the Cathedral and, removing any trace of intelligent thought from her face, stepped into the bright sun. From the corner of her eye she saw the papaya seller, pulling a wet rag over his fruit. She must decide. And fast. Before reaching the corner for to hesitate would attract attention.

She would *not* go to the Hotel Davao. She would go straight back to the University.

An hour later as students flowed out for lunch, she was parking in the No Parking zone, straight in the face of a Penalties Officer.

"Ticket me!" she smiled. He ran his brown peasant hand along the silky side of her car, watched her walk away. She was also watched by a youth without books, who leant on a pillar. A girl he knew as "Alicia" made her way towards Norma.

"Is something wrong?"

"Keep walking. *Smile"*

The youth saw them link arms and laugh.

"Have you got it?"

"Too dangerous."

"I'll go tonight."

"Don't."

"Someone has to get it."

The youth watched the girls part, fingers disentangling as they leaned away from each other, tossing heads in seeming endearment.

"All this is my father's land. 6000 hectares of bananas," Ricky gunned the pickup's engine, scattering red dust behind them. "This was a swamp before we came." His broad hand scanned the expanse of green. "Full of snakes. My father reclaimed it with prison labour."

"He believes the criminal should have the chance to reform himself," Fredo murmured.

"Why should the State feed them?" Ricky asked.

"He paid?"

"Of course. The Penal Institute is short of money."

"And cigarette money for the men," Fredo said quietly.
Abaca spikes scratched the sides of their vehicle.

"Hard work."

"Hard men."

"Who did the land belong to? Before your father?"
Ricky slowed on a bend, "As you ask, from 1565 to 1895
to Spain. Then they had a war with the Americans, the
Spanish American War. And it became a US colony.
But from the end of WW2 it's been ours. The Filipinos."

"I didn't know that," Jack said.

"Really? When my parents were kids, they had *'United
States of America'* on one side of all their coins."

"We do like the Americans," Fredo stated.

"You know they tried to annex Mindanao? From us at
independence?"

"To keep back one island?"

"One rich island."

He drummed fingers on the wheel.

Up ahead through the trees, an open sided building
could be seen.

"That's the packing shed. Want to stretch your legs?"
As they slowed, a young woman emerged from a
barracks-like building amongst coconut trees, paused,
enamel bowl on her hip, to watch them.

"She's a de-leafer. Works Monday to Saturday 6.00 to
3.00. Off duty now."
The young woman continued staring. All of 19, finely
chiselled, she bent to swat something biting her leg.

"Her ambition is probably to become a nurse. She'll be
saving from her salary."
Inside the shed women in loose cotton dresses carried
on working without looking up. They rinsed bananas in
troughs, tossing those not regulation size to one side and

packing the remainder, still green, into boxes which men were loading onto a refrigerated truck. Behind the shed arms of green bananas hooked onto cableways clanked and jostled forward like headless corpses.

"Men are out there hooking them on."

"How much is all this worth?"

"US$26 million a year." Ricky gave an infectious smile.

"Our family takes care of 7000 workers. 20,000 if you include their families. Shall we continue?"

The pickup skidded up and down hills. "This is our neighbour's. Grows pineapples."

"What about up there?" Jack pointed towards ridges covered with native forest.

"Not ours. We *could* grow up there."

"But the *Ata* tribes live there," Fredo put in.

"Ata?"

"Oh Norma can tell you all about them! How many cooking pots they've got!" Ricky scoffed. "All that! She's at university. We didn't go. But we know what we know! She'll just marry anyway."

"So what do you know?"

"That those *Atas* would have killed each if it weren't for our plantation between them!" He cornered a bend. "Whoa!"

Ahead an old Pantranco bus straddling a slurry of orange earth was gently slipping towards the road's edge, a man on the roof desperately throwing down bundles, pointing and shouting, to passengers knee deep in mud. Ricky jumped out, pulled a spade from under the seat, bent by the bus's wheels, muscles rippling, dislodging spadefuls of sludge while Fredo slashed at foliage, pushed it under the wheels, waving at the people, shouting: "Back!" The bus was settling at a new angle. Jack jumped out of the pickup.

"Leave the stuff on top!" Ricky shouted. "Leave it! Get down!" It was ballast, weighting the bus from toppling. As Jack crossed, Ricky vanished round the other side followed by men who began to rock the bus. Push squelch! Push squelch! Jack bent to push the spare tyre under a wheel, almost trapping his hand. He was slipping, sliding. A small girl ran to him, talking urgently, taking his hand, leading him away as if he were a younger child. Jack tried to free himself. The girl had the hands of a worker. What was she saying? Leave it to the men? Probably. All of eight years old and she pushed him back into the pickup, giving a most beautiful smile. He stayed. Now Fredo was standing in front of the heaving bus, directing, shouting encouragement, this way, this way, making signs at the trembling driver, the crowd now standing well back, the roar of the engine drowning the cries of a family below trying to rescue their pigs and maize plants from the descending sludge. Finally with a lurch the bus was free.

"Pineapple roots are too shallow." Ricky murmured, jumping back into the pickup. "Happens all the time."

"I was wondering," Jack asked. "Could you give me a ride into Davao City?"

"Sure. Anytime"

"Tomorrow afternoon?"

"Be too hot for *you*!"

"Tomorrow evening then."

"After dark is dangerous!"

"How about first thing tomorrow?"

"We crop spray in the morning between 5.00 and 8.00 a.m. That's why you don't see us at breakfast. It's cool then. And the wind is right. We spray three hours a day in two light planes." He turned to look at Jack, waved his arm proudly at the view beyond the window. *"Green and pleasant land!"* He grinned. "Just like your English Building Jerusalem song!"

Alicia paused. There were no lights on. The place looked desolate. She crossed the road without looking around, confident she was not being followed. Being a whorehouse, instead of a front door the Hotel Davao had an entrance men could dart quickly through without attracting attention. The lobby was deserted. Going behind the reception desk, she took a room key, opened a cupboard, lifted out a dustpan and brush, turned onto the stairwell and paused. The reek of urine burned her nostrils. Why couldn't men go outside to go to the toilet? Even if the room had one, or the woman was "doing something to herself" in it, they used the stairs. Reaching the second floor she turned right on the corridor, inserted the key in the door of the second room and coaxed it 'til the lock turned.

The room was empty, the bed sheet partly pulled back on the stained mattress of a room where men had women who were menstruating. A small table stood by the barred window, its edge pocked with cigarette burns; to one side, an electric socket hung by a thread of wire. Someone had wiped some substance on the dirty green wall and the bolt from inside the door had been removed. Otherwise all was normal. The toilet door stood partly open, with, as she knew, its empty cistern and crud infested pan. The only item out of the ordinary was the small collection of dried hair and cigarette butts in the corner where the metal waste basket *usually stood and where* ....!

As she ran to get out, in the second in which the world beyond the door, the concrete stairwell with its peeling paint and stained walls, became a longed for eternity away, she knew she was caught. She tried to control her breathing.

Efigenia watched Norma.
  "Are you alright?"
  "I need to make a phone call –"
A moment later she was back again.
  "Was your friend out?"
Norma picked at her nails.
  "I think I might go out for half an hour –"
  "We're eating at seven."
Norma went upstairs.
Efigenia took up her embroidery.
Norma came down again, sat quite close to her mother.
  "Not going out?"
  "No"

Grabbed from behind, her face forced into the toilet pan, neck pinned by a soldier's hand, Alicia heard a second soldier reach up, yank the chain, pull. Nothing. He jangled the chain. It made an empty rattling noise. To the side of the toilet she saw the legs of the missing metal chair which had alerted her too late to danger.
  "Fill the bath."
  "No plug."
The grip on her neck relaxed.

"I've come to clean the room!"

The soldier gave her a crack across the back of the neck knocking her head back into the toilet bowl. Seeing her unconscious, the first soldier climbed on the lidless rim, pulled the chain which snapped, put his hand into the cistern and lifted out an old Grundig Dictaphone. He grinned. A part-used tape was still in place.

Opening her eyes Alicia saw the soldiers by the window tinkering with the Grundig, unwinding its flex, plugging it in. She tried to get to her feet but her feet and hands were hog tied. They pressed the Fast Forward and Playback buttons, a voice whizzing at high speed then CLICK, the right speed: ".... A report of two workers, one called "Eddie" being taken in by plainclothes." The gentle tones of the elderly Irish American priest who'd stayed on and gone into hiding, his politeness, his habit of remembering peoples' names so deeply ingrained that he ignored the primary rule: never name names. Please God he wouldn't say hers! *Please God!* "Will you put Virgil Cabrera and Igmedio Daduval in Officially Disappeared please Al –" He stopped. "Thank you." A shuffling of papers then the voice continued. "Releases and Transfers – ". Alicia's spirit hovered. "Rosaline Bravo, released June 12th re-arrested two days later…" The voice paused, then picked up speed. "Original arrest in Paranaque. Juan Maniquis, apprehended May 13th in – "The voice stopped, footsteps beyond the door. When they'd passed it, it continued. " – in Bulacan, transferred from isolation to main detention centre. An Aragay man, Benito Lorena, picked up July 5, taken to Fort Bonifacio and *believed to have been transferred back down here?* Message on a dinner plate. Put a note that Myrna Corpuz was stripped naked, -" he paused as if reading with difficulty – "- a knife pointed at her belly and told – that if she wanted her baby born the normal way," the voice rushed on, "she must give the information required. That's the 182nd Philippine Constab –" the voice cut sharply, to the evident frustration of the soldiers, themselves peasants, proud to have worked out how to operate the Grundig. They replayed the last words at a slower speed where an intake of the priest's breath and a faint touch at the door could be heard, the machine being swiftly switched off as the door began to rattle.

They pulled Alicia into the room, tied her to the metal chair.

"That American priest, you know him?"

"I don't know any American priests."

"You don't know the American Missionary Fathers that got kicked out?"

"If they're kicked out, they're gone."

The first soldier rewound the tape while the second walked into the bathroom. The voice began again: "…Taloytoy Gubat – tribal farmer – suspected of being NPA –" She heard the tap running into the metal wastebasket.

"You're going to tell us where he gets his information."

"I'm a cleaner! I clean outside hours!"

"You students think you're so clever – "

The soldier straddled her knee, fixing a blindfold round her eyes, the weight of his body heavy with trespass. To her left, she heard the chinking of a bottle striking the metal bin and visualized the other soldier crouched in front of her, tapping the waste bin gently with a Coke bottle found under the bed. Tap. Tap. Tap. She had typed the details of water torture a hundred times yet had never thought it would happen to her.

"Whose was the voice?"

The blindfold was ripped off and the filthy rag, usually tied around the u-bend of the sink pipe, dipped in the bucket and hauled out, old hairs, cigarette ash and a solitary Band Aid clinging to it. It was lifted slowly to her face.

"Start talking."

They grinned at each other, pulling her head back by the hair, laying the cloth on her face, tipping water over it so she gasped for breath. One soldier pushed her in the stomach then when she opened her mouth, tipped more water.

"Great meal, thank you."

"Please eat here until your – domestic arrangements are finalised," Victor coaxed.

"Pass Father Jack's coffee, Norma."

"Coffee, Jack."

"*Father* Jack," Efigenia hissed quietly.

"I need to learn *Tagalog* – " Jack began.

Efigenia opened her hands: "But everyone here speaks English – (!)"

"Except the tribespeople," Norma added. "Of whom there are several thousand."

"*That is enough!*"

"He may as well know the truth. Or some of it."

"Norma is a student."

"English is the medium of education in our schools," Efigenia continued. "We have so *many* languages it *has* to be!"

"We think in English," Victor added.

"There are some things *I* think in *Tagalog.*"

"Like what?" a younger child asked Norma.

"We don't want to know thank you!"

"Son of a bitch!" The soldier slapped Alicia across the face, tipped more water. She began to choke under the cloth. He signed the other. They completely stopped moving. Silence. Alicia's eyeballs moved under the cloth, her mouth grasping for air. Grinning, the one soldier lifted the bottle, gently twanged it against the metal bin, made splashing noises in the water with his fingers.

"Help me! Help!"

They poured more water.

"I'm not Alicia!"

The first soldier ripped off the wet towel.

"Who mentioned an Alicia?"

Alicia started to sob and moan

"She's the bitch who types the Detainee Situationers!" the second soldier said.

Choking on tears Alicia dipped her head.

"We're wasting time – " He pulled off her finger ring and watch and pocketed them, slapped her across the face with the wet towel, emptied the bin onto her upturned face, holding her head back by the hair, forcing her jaw so that water ran up her nose into her mouth.

"What is it to you? We've got him!"

"It is every Filipino mother's dearest wish to have a son who is a priest," Efigenia insisted.

"When they have five others who aren't"

"Ignore Norma."

"You will not find a more devout country. For us, Sunday is a special day. How many countries can say that? We dress up and go to church together – as a

31

family.   The priest here is the most loved, the most popular man in the village."

Alicia struggled for breath.
  "I'll tell you!"
The water stopped.
  "I'm cleaning for another girl!"
  "She only wants to breathe!" He kicked her in the face. "What'll you put this time? 'Grieving Relatives Unable to Claim American Priest's Body for Burial?'"
  "If we didn't" Alicia shouted "who would?"
Crash! The soldier swung his rifle butt breaking her neck.

  As they hurried down the stairs, behind his unlit door, the proprietor listened. He came out when they'd gone, checked the lobby and street beyond, then moved up the stairs and listened at the door, opened it a crack. Directly in his line of vision he could see Alicia strapped to the chair. Ignoring her he ran to the mattress, trying to force his crushed fingers in the slit.   Grasping his left hand round his right wrist, using his hand as a shovel, his fingers touched paper.   Thank God!   They were there! She had not spoken!   *Because she had not known!* Drawing out the notes scribbled on scraps, he hastily pushed them between his singlet and thin chest and ran out leaving the light on.   Dawn would come up on the torn leaves of the *plantain* beyond the barred window, the tropical clouds would gather and pass on, but the girl on the chair would never move again.

As 10.30 approached Norma phoned Alicia's mother. "Is she home yet?" she asked.
  "No. Do you know where she went?"
  "Maybe to a party -?"

She hung up.

Alicia's parents would be too frightened. They would never phone the police.

Chapter Three

Norma did not appear at breakfast.

"Sometimes she eats with the little ones," Efigenia explained. "Or with Ricky and Fredo when they get back from spraying. Do you have plans for today?"

"I'm anxious to stop being a professional guest –"

"When the children's driver gets back I'll be going out to the Shrine. Perhaps –"

Norma entered.

"Where's the paper?"

"Do you want to read it?"

"Why should I? It's full of lies."

She stomped out to the balcony where Victor was sipping his orange juice, the *Mindanao Post* and the *Mindanao Journal* beneath his chair. She stopped.

Victor put his juice down, turned his eyes full on her.

"Have you – *heard* anything?" she asked.

"About?"

"About – things in general – "

"There is no talk."

Jack watched Norma pacing about. She stopped and glared at him. "Are you thinking I'm a 'poor little rich girl'?" She waited for him to respond.

"I'm here because your parents are letting me stay 'til my quarters are ready -" Jack said blandly.

"You can move out tomorrow."

"Why would I throw your parents' kindness back in their face?"

"*Kindness?* My mother's perhaps. Be ready in five minutes and I'll drive you to the Cathedral and get you set up! See if you like being a priest!"

Five minutes later Norma marched past Jack swinging her car keys. "Ready?" She was wearing a classic dress, with high *terno* sleeves reminiscent of their Spanish past.

"Don't you have a dog-collar?"

"In this heat?"

"I'd prefer you look like a priest if you are to be seen with me." She opened her car door. "Definitely not shorts with those fuzzy legs. Go and change."

"Should I tell anyone I'm going?"

"Hurry."

Once in the car she ignored him, lost in thought, driving slower and slower.

"Do you always drive in second?" Jack asked. No response. "Your mind isn't on the driving."

"Will you be quiet? I'm thinking."

Nearing town they bumped over a rickety bridge, its sides shored up with P.S.P. from the Second World War. A ripe smell arose from the mud and muddy water lapped the mangrove roots, swilled the stilts of shacks from which children stared, their rags drying on sticks.

"Phew!"

"That's mud. Not sewage."

"What a place to live!"

"It's very good for crabbing at night. And shrimps. They comb the mud and lure the crayfish with lights."

She reached in her bag for her sunglasses, placed them carefully on her nose and as they entered town, switched on the radio, becoming suddenly bright and alert.

She parked. "This is it, the only modern store in town. Do you want to buy tissues or something?"

"A postcard?"

"You think a place like this has *postcards?* We don't even have tourists! Not with Martial Law. What's to see here anyway?" She slammed the car into Park. "*You're here by special arrangement.*"

Uncertain as to her mood, Jack climbed out. Suddenly she beamed as if they were the best of friends.

"Parking can be difficult at the Cathedral so I leave my car all over the place. Come." She smiled warmly.

Jack followed into the store and straight out the back.

"This way."

As they passed behind a newspaper office and turned into a side street, Jack felt her false energy crystallize into fear. Unaware, she had taken hold of his arm, her fingers dug into him. He could feel her shaking. Ahead on the other side of the street a small knot of people were lingering outside a shabby building.

"Stay back!" she whispered, pulling at him. "Stop! Stop!"

Under a blanket, a stiff shape on a chair was being carried towards a police van, its doors open, passers-by slowing, but careful not to stop. On the edge of the group a frantic looking man was trying to hold back a woman. Jack felt Norma move slightly behind him.

"She has been dumped here!" the woman shouted.

"Shut up!" the man urged, pulling her back.

"This is a whorehouse!"

The man reached forward gratefully to take a shoulder bag from a policeman who was following the body out. "Thank you Officer. Girls can't tell who their clients are these days," he apologised, trying to push his wife up the street. She punched him, shouted:

"She was a decent girl!"

Jack felt himself turned around, pulled back the way they had come by Norma, breathing loudly, walking without a purpose. Finally she stopped, leant against a wall, pulling him in front of her as if to hide. He took her shoulder:

"Do you want to sit down?"

"Don't mention this to my parents."

"You're in shock. Let me get you a drink - "

He tried to lead her towards a cafe.

"I can't go in there!"

Gradually her breathing calmed, but she stayed close to the wall.

"Do you want to go home?"

She shook her head, started walking again.

Finally the Cathedral came into view.

"I need time to myself," she said quietly.

Jack wandered around the cool, dark cathedral wondering where were the rooms that Victor said were being refurbished for him. He went outside and followed the outline finding, towards the back on the right-hand side, a wall protruding at right angles. Were the rooms behind it? The door in the wall was firmly locked and seemed to have been so for eons.

He re-entered the Cathedral, passed Norma, still at the back, face buried in her hands, went to the front of the Cathedral and found what he took to be the corresponding door leading to the suite of rooms. As he tried the handle, a throat was cleared behind him.

"Can I help you?"

It was the man who had prevented him from entering the Cathedral the first time and driven him instead to the Salcedos.

"Is this the suite of rooms that's being refurbished for me?"

"How did you come here?"

Jack pointed towards Norma at the rear of the Cathedral. The Sacristan's face adjusted.

"Excuse me."

He walked back to Norma and waited politely 'til she looked up.

"Excuse me Miss Salcedo but what is the intention?"

In one of Norma's sudden changes, which Jack was beginning to recognise as part of her character, she flashed him a disarming smile and rose to her feet, at once the lady and patroness.

"Would you kindly unlock the rooms Reynaldo? Father Jack wishes a preview."

The man turned, headed back up the aisle fumbling amongst his keys, inserting one, turning the handle, then putting his shoulder to the door which gave with a splintering sound, plaster falling around them as they stepped through.

"I would like you to borrow a frame bed, a table and two chairs from the nuns, hire a truck and charge it to my father. Have the place washed and cleaned. Father Jack will move in on Friday."

"Yes Miss Norma."

"And he'll be saying the 9.30 Mass on Sunday. Put it on the notice board."

The Sacristan withdrew.

"What a tip!"

Plaster shed from broken lathes hanging from the ceiling dappled the floor; birds had nested above the windows, their feathers and scrapes decked ledges, their droppings hardened on the floor.

"Phoar!" Norma covered her nose.

Coughing, Jack pushed at a shuttered window which gave with a loud crack, dislodging a nest which fell, expelling an egg to break at his feet.

"Next to your altar, the pigeon finds a place to build her nest." Jack quoted, the frantic bird flying round his head.

"There's an omen for you."

He walked into the kitchen.

"Has this place ever been used?"

"Not actually. And it'll fly in the face of Filipino hospitality, my parents allowing you to stay here –"

"I'm moving in – " Jack forced the kitchen screen door which gave onto a small yard. Outside the air was fresh and shade provided by a giant banyan tree whose roots were undermining the kitchen's foundations.

"You'll need a metal screen for security."

"I've nothing of value –"

"Still – " Norma led the way back through the musty smelling rooms, closed the door.

"He won't hire a van. His brother-in-law'll do it and they'll split the charge."

Leaving the Cathedral, she walked silently in front of Jack as if he were not there. In the car she became further detached, pulling off her shades, driving slower and slower.

"Are we going home?"

"No."

"Do you want to talk?"

"No."

But she stopped the car and they sat. Finally, she began driving very slowly. Unconsciously Jack hummed *Bridge Over Troubled Water* but seeing her trying to hide tears, fell silent. They were now some distance from town on a track separated by a belt of coconut trees from a narrow strip of beach, its sand unmarked but for waterlogged coconuts and fallen palm fronds, a shallow sea glistening beyond. She parked abruptly, got out, pointed ahead at a cluster of dwellings on a wider spur of beach.

"Do you know what that is?"

"Fishing village?"

"Those are people," she said looking at Jack as if it were his fault, "that my father, and others like him, have made homeless." She began walking towards it, feet sinking in the sand. "Farmers. Dumped here and told to fish. The same week the Justice Department ruled multinationals could trawl off our shore."

Jack waited.

"They are squeezing out the local fisheries that we are trying to get to help the newcomers."

"We?"

"The Share and Care Apostolate for Poor Settlers. SCAPS."

The slum settlement came into view.

"Those people," Norma said, pointing at another group, "were booted out of their homes to make way for a chemical plant."

"Here?"

"It was moved here from Chiba City in Japan because it caused respiratory disease. And death. Give the citizens of Chiba Prefecture credit: they protested when it was relocated rather than destroyed. Our pollution laws aren't stringent." She indicated a man resting on the door of a hut half sunk in sand: "He used to grow food. Now he must buy." The man stared long-sightedly out to sea, torn shorts fluttering in the wind. "With what? Hey!" she shouted. "An *Englishman* for you to meet! A priest!"

"I could help here - rebuilding - "

"Why? This beach will become an Export Processing Zone making Barbie dolls with cheap labour. They want a priest. But don't go on about the blessedness of being poor to people who've lost everything for the sin of getting in the way of a developer."

By now people were clustering around them.

"Father! Are you going to say Mass?"

"Come in and have lunch!"

"Bless us!"

"If they're so poor maybe we shouldn't eat – "

"I should have thought that was the whole point!"

"Come in! Move around everyone! Sit!"

A child was sent running and a plate of cold rice arrived, followed by what looked like a boiled egg.

"*Balut!* What an honour!"

"*Balut! Balut!*" the children chirped.

"Go on!" Norma urged. *"Bite it."*

"Get Father a beer –"

Jack turned the egg in his hands. The children shrieked.

"Bite it," Norma prompted. "It's an almost hatched chicken's egg!"

Jack moved his thumbs warily against the egg's surface.

A little girl snatched it from his hands, snapped off the shell, thrust it back at him. They waited expectantly.

"Father doesn't like *balut*!"

"Have a bite Father! Try!" an old man nodded encouragement from the doorway. The children's eyes became curious as Jack raised the egg to his mouth.

"AAah!"

It had vanished! Jack searched his fingers mystified, looked up at the roof, down at the floor. Where had it gone? By the time a child found it up his sleeve, all were at ease.

"In our case," said a man with cavernously thin chest. "We were offered compensation but our village was divided on whether to take it. A man from Manila assessed our buildings, our smallholding crops. It was all done very properly and there were many who advised us. At first we held out for higher compensation. Except for a group who followed the advice of -" he looked at Norma who frowned, changed tack "- those who did not agree that we should leave. But we here disassembled our houses, laid them in neat piles by the road as we had been told for the Company transport trucks. Any house left standing would be bulldozed. With or without occupants. We understood that."

The room was quiet.

"The truck came –"

The children's eyes were on the narrator. "We got on and were taken to an elementary school not far from here. It was the school holidays so we could sleep there. We did not receive compensation. No one delivered our housing materials –."

The room fell silent.

"What about those who stayed behind?"

"We have not been back to see."

As they walked from the village, Norma's mood changed.

"You've come to a whorehouse," she muttered. "When a rich nation comes calling, we check their credit then let them in. Ferdinand Marcos is the bloated Madam in the parlour." She pulled clothing, rope and a groundsheet from the car, passed them to a man who had accompanied them and took off, continually checking her rear-view mirror.

"That was a good thing you did."

"SCAPS is a proscribed organization. Don't associate with it."

"Because of your father?"

She turned the radio on. Jack turned it off.

"Why shouldn't I? I think it's a good idea."

"It's for students."

"And?"

"Well *obviously,*" she looked at him as if he were a complete child. "It's infiltrated. You'd be putting yourself in danger. OK?"

They continued in silence. After a while she pulled the car over.

"What are you doing here?"

"This is an overseas posting. We've always served in the Missions in Africa. This is American Missionary territory so -"

"The Americans were good."

"This is a new thing for us."

"Who invited you?"

"The government. Which is presumably why the Filipino Church has not made contact."

Norma's eyes widened. She drove home without saying another word.

At the foot of the hill leading to Mansion Salcedo, she stopped. "You can get out here. Don't say where you've been -"

"I can hardly lie - "

"We'll see." She let in the clutch, roared up the hill.

"We were worried! Where have you been?" Efigenia cried, walking towards them.

"Round and about." Norma said passing her. Efigenia clasped her hands. "I'm fussing! There's something I'd like to show you, if you have a moment."

Jack followed her to an upstairs room where the eldest of the child maids, fourteen-year-old Loretta, was seated at a sewing machine, pieces of cloth spread on the floor round her.

"Loretta is learning to sew!" Efigenia beamed, her hand on the young girl's shoulder. "In her free time in the afternoons. Show Father what you've done."

Loretta picked up a skirt and held it out.

"See how well she's done the gathering? Now which piece goes with that?" Loretta picked up the bodice. Efigenia hugged her absently.

"It's one of Norma's dresses. Loretta is making a first dance dress for herself, a skirt for Angela and a pinny for Ninette so they won't feel left out. They grow so quickly!"

She summoned Jack to the back window where below on the step Angela, 12, and Ninette, 9, sat playing a kind of five-stones. Efigenia tapped on the window. They looked up. The trickling sound of the sewing machine filled the room.

"You have taken on these children?"

"It is expected."

"Will you send them to college?"

"To own her own sewing machine will have vastly exceeded any expectations Loretta's parents had for her at birth."

Efigenia took a couple of sideways steps.

"I wouldn't tell Victor you spent the morning with Norma if I were you."

"Suppose he asks?"

"You'll find he won't."

During the meal Jack sensed Norma trying to put him on the spot, as if he'd crossed some kind of divide and she'd changed her opinion of him. She needled him, prodding, provoking until he said straight out:

"I've been extremely happy here -"

"You want to leave!"

"I came to work as a priest -."

"But your settling-in period -"

"So when are you moving out?" Victor asked bluntly.

"Friday."

"Happy for you. Congratulations."

Jack continued eating, feeling Norma curl her lip. Ricky and Fredo talked plantation. Efigenia alone was upset.

"Will you come and visit?"

"Often."

Victor got up, fetched the cognac.

"There's something *I'd* like to show you -."

Pulling on a pair of Fredo's boots, Jack followed Victor through scrub to a paddock on the edge of an *ipil-ipil* plantation. He paused, hand on a stable door.

"What do you think I've got in here?"

At first Jack could only make out a small black and white cat, then, behind it, an utterly beautiful horse.

"Good Lord!"

Victor laid a hand on Jack's shoulder.

"I knew you'd appreciate it."

"I'm amazed!"

"I have had people here who see nothing special about this horse."

"A thoroughbred. No mistaking it."

Victor exhaled slowly.

"Do you ride?"

"No. You?"

"No. She's standoffish. But loves that cat. They are companions."

The horse watched Jack crouch, extending a hand towards the cat, who raised her tail and went immediately to him.

"I want to make a cardboard box factory here," Victor said dreamily. "The cost of a box is higher than the fruit it packs. Because the technology is complicated," he paused. "Even if we could import liner board and corrugated medium our agreements with customers like Japan restrict us to shipping our goods in their cartons." He shook his head. "Our boxes collapse before arriving." He sighed. "Sophisticated machinery is needed. But *one day* I will make this technology available to the people of Mindanao." He looked at the horse. "And possibly, to the Philippines as a whole. One day," he said, eyes though not hand resting on the horse's neck, "there will be a plant here on my land producing 90 million cardboard boxes a year. We will no longer import them from Taiwan or buy back from the Japanese the reassembled wood pulp they bought from us! One day – we will *not* be an exporter of raw materials!"

"How did you clear your land of people to establish your banana plantation?" Jack asked bluntly.

Victor looked stunned.

He stepped outside.

"I am not an evil man. My land is not cleared of people. That crescent of hills has been left entirely to the *Atas* -."

"Who are hemmed in and could hardly leave - "

"The reason they do not leave is because there is nowhere for them to go. I let them stay -."

"*Let* them?"

"I am helping them integrate! I buy *ipil-ipil* from them. *I* taught them to plant it. I don't need theirs: I grow it myself! Look around you." He began to walk rapidly towards the house. "The leaves contain protein, calcium, magnesium, potassium, nitrogen, phosphorous. You think I should not have introduced the *Ata* to commercial crops? We make fertilizer from *ipil-ipil*; grind it for pig feed. The stems make props. How would they know *ipil-ipil*? It was brought here from Mexico by the Spaniards."

"I'm not say – "

"Not only are the *Ata* on *my* land –" Victor continued. "But in that crescent between the hills – the *Atas,* you see, prefer the hilltops – are common, ordinary settlers from the Visayas. The Visayas are the islands to the North of Mindanao."

"But much of your land cannot have been empty -."

"And I had always thought priests were prepared to see the best in their fellow man," Victor said sadly.

They reached the house in silence.

"If you would come into the study," Victor invited, "you may inspect our Management Agreements." He pulled sheafs of paper from a desk drawer: "These are – supplied to us – by the legal division of *Del Mundo* -." He passed one to Jack. " – and as you see, once an existing settler has signed, he still owns his land but we manage it for him."

Jack read.

"In exchange for the use of their land for a period of initially – fifteen years, we offer them 18 cents American for every carton of bananas produced on their land. Is that fair?"

"It's all in English -."

"Would you prefer *Boholano? Tagalog? Bagabo, Ilocano?* I allow the C.C.J.P. and a multitude of other services who make a living by sowing the seeds of discontent and mistrust amongst their fellow men to advertise their free legal services in my packing sheds. They translate and advise. I don't interfere. I don't deny there are settlers who think they will own a car and TV within one week – off the backs of their fellow workers. They imagine they will make a dollar a minute! The fact, of course, is – and it is as plain as the nose on your face – that, in order for us to grow this mutually shared and beneficial crop, they are required to vacate the land."

Jack was up to page three: "I see here -"

"They can, of course," Victor interrupted "make capital while not living on the land – well, not living *all over the land* but in designated areas – by working in the plantation as plantation workers at a dollar and a half a day."

"And out of this will come the costs of production." Jack read. "Correct me if I'm wrong, but does that mean that at the end of the fifteen years, out of the accumulated profits must come the labourers' wages, the chemicals, the fertilizer, seedlings, the *ipil-ipil* props… the cost of buildings, machinery, irrigation ditches, roads …"

"Of course."

"- because if so, some of these people would end up in debt -."

"Nobody gets anything for nothing." Victor paused. "Not me. Not anyone. At the end of fifteen years they renew their contracts." He looked at Jack. *"I have made these people partners in development.* They have access to healthcare, education, sports, electricity, consumer goods – ."

"What about those who won't move?"

"We Filipinos may be idealists but we accept reality. Few of us want to put the clock back."

He cocked his head slightly. "I left school at fourteen and started out in an automobile repair shop in Manila." He recalled the dud batteries, the oil slicked floors. "That's why that horse means so much to me."

Jack remembered the woman in the black dress.

"Do your men use violence?"

"If I find a man who does, he will answer to me!"

"And what if a family won't leave?"

"Usually it's enough to park the Range Rovers opposite their holdings for a day or two ..."

"Here you are!" Efigenia exclaimed. "I had given up on you!" Her eyes scanned the Management Contracts on Victor's desk. "Oh! The 'face savers'," she smiled. "Half of these people don't have title to their land at all!"

Jack returned his copy to Victor's desk: "I hope you don't think -."

"Far from it!" Victor beamed. "He was showing concern for our people," he explained to Efigenia. "It is what we expect and want from you."

"That's right Father," Efigenia nodded. "Don't hold back. If there's anything you think we could or should be doing better, please tell us!"

"I know nothing about – the way things work. You must excuse me. I don't even speak the language."

"You will! And you will be wonderful! I know it!"

Jack stepped from the room.

Victor slid the Contracts together.

"He is naive and stupid."

"Victor!"

"He can take his big mouth elsewhere."

"I will not have you upsetting him," Efigenia's eyes filled. "Away from home, a guest with no one to turn to - ."

"Who does he think he is, coming here inspecting our Contracts?"

"He's a young man like Fredo and Ricardo. His opinions are still being formed. You should be pleased he turned to you instead of - well - Others..."

"When I think of the patience I used on those blood mongering *Atas!* This one boasting he should be chief, because he's more powerful than the military, the NPA - ."

"Sssh!"

" - the MNLF! That if people didn't obey him he'd have their heads off! Bickering, raiding each other for kickbacks- (!) They're bent as snakes!"

"You're always fair, I know that. I'm sure he didn't mean -"

"I'll tell you one thing. If he carries on the way he's doing, he'll end up strung up like that American priest -"

"!Surely they - "

"My information is one of them didn't leave with the rest of the Order."

"That can't be true!"

"One of his ears was mailed to the Bishop."

Jack tapped on the door to Norma's room. She was seated at her desk.

"I think you'd better stop interpreting the political situation for me," he said to her back.

"Read this yourself then."

She handed him a report printed on cheap paper.

"I'm not reading that."

"So you are not interested in knowing the amount of militarism and torture necessary to keep Western supermarket shelves stocked?"

"I'm interested in people. Not rhetoric."

"Oh fine then!" She snatched back the manuscript. "Just thought you'd like to know that this, *The Mindanao Report,* which is about *people,* is the reason the American Missionary Fathers were kicked out. We have people - on pineapple plantations – whose day's wage can't buy a tin of pineapple juice!"

"That's a collection of statistics!"

"Which shows the foreign exchange the giant agri-businesses earn goes overseas and is of no benefit to the Filipino people –" Norma shouted, "who've been made slaves in their own country!"

"Your father," said Jack, louder than he'd meant, "is managing an enterprise where, without titled right, settlers have secure employment and are encouraged to feel part of the developmental effort."

"Well that's fine then!" She unfolded her arms, pushed the door in his face.

Jack went back to the study. Victor was alone.

"I overstepped the mark earlier -."

"It doesn't do to go off half-cocked in this country -."

"I don't intend to become involved in -" Not *social justice.* What was the word?

"Be your own man." Victor said, looking him straight in the eye. "Don't step into anyone else's shoes."

"I'm not here to make trouble - "

"Any ideas you need to chew over before – forming opinions – consider my ear open -."

"I appreciate that."

"Be particularly careful in your first sermon – not to be swayed by considerations that might not – sit well. Stay on the fence."

"I will."

"A lack of criticism, in this country, does not mean people agree with you. Avoid complex issues," he paused. "Because a person will not challenge you until they are in a position to wipe you out."

"I'll try to remember."

"I hope so my boy because that is the best advice I can give."

Chapter Four

Crack! Emerenciana opened her eyes. She had been sleeping at the Shrine a week now and did not want to be caught by the foreman, whom she could see a few yards from where she lay swiping at shoots which had dared to grow half an inch during the night. *Swish* went his *parang*. *Clang!* It dispatched a stone. His dark feet, cracked and yellowed at the edges, moved closer, toes far apart, the largest with a great wide nail. *Crick!* His heel crushed a leaf. He passed, cut grass stuck to his ankles. She heard him clear his throat, spit.

She had been dreaming of a childhood visit to an aunt's, when her whole family had gone on the journey, not more than 30 miles as the crow flies but lasting two nights. The part she'd been remembering was the cramped inside of the PU where she'd sat opposite two young men dressed as ladies, their long painted nails clicking on their knees as they talked in concerned voices about a party they were going to. When they'd stopped in a local hamlet, the driver had bought them cold drinks and people had whistled and called in a friendly way, but the women travellers hadn't talked to them.

Emerenciana splashed her face in a puddle and went into the Shrine. Although the Shrine was to the Infant – she could read the word "Infant" – it was always to the Virgin that Emerenciana prayed and sometimes the Sacred Heart, taking care to remind Him that in the house where her family had recently been massacred an image of the Sacred Heart had been clearly displayed on the wall, with beneath it the words: "I will bless the house wherein the image of my Sacred Heart is displayed."

She knelt, thanking the Sacred Heart for finding her a good place to leave ten-year-old Wilma. They had been in Davao market looking for scraps when a woman, about her own age, had caught her attention. She'd watched the woman picking through tomatoes, selecting those almost but not quite off, bargaining vigorously. The woman had a large basket. She'd put the heavy items at the bottom, so the tomatoes, going on top, would be her last purchase. Water dripped from the basket. That meant fish. The woman must be shopping for a large family on a daily basis and, given the food was about to go off, was not a maid. She wore an old pair of American jeans which bulged at the zip and a white t-shirt with words written on it, probably passed on from a son in work somewhere. As she bent to pick up her basket Emerenciana pushed Wilma forward.

The woman looked up at the thin ten-year-old reaching for the handle of her basket, the dark serious eyes in the oval face, the home cut hair and blotchy skin typical of a child grown up with mosquitoes. She also reached for her basket. The little grip did not relax.

The woman looked around, saw Emerenciana watching. The child's paper thin dress was carefully stitched with no cloth wasted on frills or pockets. She nodded. Wilma wrenched at the huge basket, squatting as if it were a child and getting it on her hip without spilling the contents. Emerenciana came forward. Wilma rested the basket on a wall watched her mother take the other woman's hand, raise it to her lips. Then she followed the woman without turning to look back.

Now Emerenciana reasoned with the Virgin. "Please suggest to Adan that he try to find work as a newspaper vendor. He won't think of it and I don't want him falling in with bad boys. Watch him for me…"

Behind her Efigenia stepped into the Shrine, waited for her eyes to adjust. A pssp pssp was coming from the darkness. She knew it would be the woman who came daily to pray, something familiar about her but she couldn't place it. She moved to light the first votives.

The Shrine had been grudgingly blessed but the Bishop had been unwilling to give permission for Masses to be said there. Perhaps the English priest…? Really it needed a miracle. *Perhaps this very woman with her devoutness* would be the occasion for the needed miracle?! If her petition, whatever it was, were granted!? What, she wondered, did the woman pray for?

Conscious of her whistling teeth Emerenciana tried to address the Virgin more quietly. She felt ashamed for never having lit a candle, especially as she made repeated detailed requests for her grandchildren. There was the Señora, putting a magnificent cloak, sparkling with red stones on the statue. How fine it was to be able to *give* something. She patted the gaps in her teeth. This lady could very easily have kept the stones for herself. If she were rich her grandchildren could have dressed up and played Kings and Queens in that cloak! At all events she could certainly have got money for it. But no, she had spent her time, had cut and stitched the little cloak from deep, richly coloured material and somehow managed to stick the stones on. Emerenciana imagined her working the hem, beautifully done, covering the stitching with the attractive border. Pulling out 2 of her long wiry hairs, Emerenciana took her wedding ring off, threaded the hairs through the ring, knotted and looped it over the statue's head.

"Why did you do that?" Efigenia asked as Emerenciana stepped out into the sun.

"My situation, Señora," Emcrenciana explained. "Is that I need a lot of help from the Virgin. And of course the Infant." She hurriedly added, explaining her predicament. "I know God will watch over my family but I am more comfortable asking the Virgin to help as she is his mother and can suggest to him and being a mother herself, if I don't think of things, she will and can put her arms around my grandchildren, wherever they are, and suggest to them. She can whisper in the ear of people they approach and soften their hearts."

Efigenia questioned her.

"What exactly do you pray for?"

"My problem, Señora, and what I am praying for, is to find my grandchildren."

"Are they lost?"

"We were chased from our land. Adan is 14, Violetta – just 11 and Edgar, 7. Baby Cresmalin is eight months old -."

"A baby!?"

"They were still with me -." Emerenciana grasped Efigenia's wrists, leaned towards her. "All except Adan and Edgar who'd run away. It was because I went back."

"You went back?" Efigenia looked puzzled.

"We were attacked. At our evening meal. I went into town to report it and seek help. Then I went back. To bury them. My husband, my son – his wife –."

"To bury them?!"

"They were on the ground - moving. I thought they were alive. I ran at them. They – the children - couldn't take their eyes off them. Violetta was holding baby Cresmalin, Wilma was behind her. They watched me run

56

forward. As I bent to their mother – my daughter-in-law - she rolled over to face me! I screamed, jumped back! Their father, Robencio, my son, rolled towards me from my other side! It was the gas inside them Señora, the gas in their bowels moving about. And the sun. They were swollen up, heaving and rumbling! I was screaming. The children were terrified! And the smell - their bowels were emptying - bodies exploding! The noise! I turned to the children – -" she stopped. "They'd fled - all except Wilma –"

"God help you!"

"I called. We called. Four nights – with Wilma – just Wilma. To bury them all. By day we called the children. We cut through the bushes. It's so dense you cannot see a few yards. Sounds are cut off. We buried the bodies. After a week we reached here."

Efigenia looked serious: "And you are sure those of your family who are not dead are lost?"

"I watched the sky for vultures -." Efigenia dropped onto the cement bench. Emerenciana sat next to her.

"What happened to your land once you had left it?"

"It was only a tiny piece Señora."

"Had you been asked to move?"

The woman shook her head.

"Nobody visited you or parked outside your holding?"

"We were not on the road."

"Where did you say the place was?"

"It had no name. It was not yet even a place."

"And you'd been there two years?"

The woman nodded.

"I don't know how to help you." Efigenia murmured.

"You have no money –"

"Of course not."

"Did your husband survive?"

Emerenciana shook her head.

"I could have placed him on -" Efigenia felt a compunction to avoid mentioning Salcedo or the plantation.

"My husband is in Heaven -."

"The best you can do is to ask the Church. I know no other way to trace your family. I shall pray you find your grandchildren."

"You recall that woman that came to our house" Efigenia began firmly when she got home. "I mean to get to the bottom of what happened to her."

"That will never happen."

"Things cannot go on like this!"

"What do you want me to do? Reincarnate her family? Reinstate her on the land? You know that is not possible."

"I don't know *what* I'm asking."

"That I give her more land? How will she farm it? Without menfolk?"

"What is *happening* to our country?"

"Somebody has chased her off the land because they wanted it."

"But who?"

"How will it help you to know?"

"You are one of the most powerful men in Mindanao. Surely -."

"I give you my word, I have no idea."

"Can you not -."

"One stone can dislodge a spider from its web. Another spider moves in. If the web collapses, we all fall."

"Well," Efigenia said, regrouping, "We should do more for those we *can* help. I've often asked you -"

"One day, I will provide free medical and dental care on the plantation, a bowling arcade, scholarships to university, a Miss S.D.C.I. competition...."

"Not one day Victor. *Now!*" She pulled him into their bedroom. "Kneel down beside me and pray!" She knelt before her favourite picture, Our Lady of Perpetual Succour. "We have so *much* Victor." Victor felt the intensity of her devotion as she said her favourite prayer of petition, the *Memorare*.... Getting up, wet eyed, she turned to him.

"You provide *so* well. Things have been stable for such a long time -."

"I'll see what I can do."

He strode about then went into his study. No harm finding out. He picked up the phone.

"Ernesto? How are you? The family? Mm, mm. Have you heard anything? What? About anyone expressing an interest in the land." He listened. "No, I don't expect it to change anything. What?"

"You know my boundaries. I know yours."

"This is somewhere off the road - -"

"What land is there left unplanted this side of -?"

"But if something's starting up? It was only the one family but -"

"Your fault then for suggesting limiting the land planted out for export bananas so as to get some control over the price."

"Don't joke."

"Whose joking? Presidential Decree number goodness-knows-what, as you well know and you were very pleased with yourself at the time, states that any land not planted out by the end of November must be left. You created a rush!"

"This was soldiers."

"So it was soldiers," Ernesto's voice sounded bored. "You recall the last storm in a teacup? On Samar? Some battalion of soldiers doing well out of a land clearance? Lined people up on one side of the street, robbed their houses, lined them on the other side. Ditto. Shooting at random. Burnt a few huts, harvested and sold the crops - in other words, subsidised their income. Remember?"

"That was different - "

"How? The point, Victor, is that the land remained safe. Back of it was a government department ordering the land cleared so the Australians could put in a - in inverted commas - road. A pan-Highway from one end of the archipelago to the other. Of course there was no intention of building it. But large lumps of fat could be cut from loans in the name of land preparation. It all returned to normal. Everyone was happy!"

"You've become cynical Ernesto -"

"How so? The object of the exercise – from the position of those who stood to profit - was the getting of foreign aid tied to the purchase of earth moving equipment from the donor country. Global money. Millions of dollars getting released in the name of feasibility. Changing hands... So cut the dumb blonde Victor. This is normal. Things are fine. Quit worrying."

"Nevertheless – for my wife's sake - "

"Ever the gentleman! OK. I'll ask around. My nephew's godfather is a doorman at the Manila International. Sees the comings and goings. And the taxis. He has contacts."

"Mind you it is only the one family -."

"You owe me. Stay in touch."

Father Tomas finished saying the 10am Thursday Mass, conscious of a woman watching him.

As he left the altar, she rose, followed him into the robing room.

"Close the door. What can I do for you?"

"I need help to find my family."

"Write down their names, ages, the date and what happened. Be quick."

"What is your name Father?"

"That doesn't matter."

"So I can pray for you."

He handed her a scrap of paper.

"Write quickly."

"Can't write, Father."

He glanced at his watch. "Your husband's name?"

"Rustico Posa-Dominado."

"How do you spell that? Stop -!"

Emerenciana stopped speaking.

"Only me -." The Sacristan put his head in, saw Emerenciana and withdrew. When she had finished the priest looked at his disguised handwriting, folded the paper very small and sunk it deep into his pocket.

"Where are you living?"

"Nowhere."

He took some change from his pocket. "For the bus. There is a place on a beach where you might find help -"

"We were attacked-."

"There are people there -" He could not put anything more in his own writing. "I think you can find people to help you -"

When the woman had gone he unfolded, looked at the paper. Since the incident at Hotel Davao the notes had mounted up and he dared not ask about the empty pew.

"Ahum."

He turned to see the sacristan in the open door.

"Come in."

The man crossed to the bureau and placed a sack on it.

"The Mass Offerings from the back -."

"Just leave it there," the priest said sharply but the sacristan upended the sack and began separating its contents into peso notes, coin, Mass requests. Ignoring him, the priest hung his chasuble in the closet, conscious of the sacristan watching him.

"You may leave. I shall lock up."

Brother Tomas counted to five, then uncurled the first note: ".... family were massacred as they ate supper in Tinambacan, Calbayog..." He quickly folded it and half opened another: "...buses were allowed to leave on condition...."

He placed the notes requesting Masses for the Repose of Souls, for Anniversaries, Special Intentions into the Mass book and stood holding the remainder. How had the Poor Box come to be the illicit mail drop used by the wronged? In the days before martial law, if people had a problem they went to their congressman or mayor. Now they trusted only that breed of men to whom silence was a profession.

He locked the sacristy door, drew from the bureau a stand-by chalice of unconsecrated hosts. Pushing hosts aside, he slipped the notes underneath, opened the door leading onto the sanctuary, crossed to a side altar and with a small key taken from his key ring, lifted the heavy cope, unlocked the tabernacle door and slipped the chalice inside, praying that God would tell him where to hide them tomorrow. He glanced down the darkened church. Where men would turn informer for the price of a can of beer, the problem of knowing who had been "bought" was real.

Jack moved through the market, between mounds of fruit, savouring the feeling of plenty. A woman tidied her herbs, laid out like ribbons, snapped off a grape, held it out to him. He stopped to look at an enormous cabbage.

"Milk-fed Father. Called Shanghai!"

The owner quickly peeled back the outer leaves to show the firm white head, offered it, nodding encouragement with a toothy grin. Jack shook his head. The man pointed behind him at avocados glistening green and maroon; pushed aside arms of plantains to show his scrubbed potatoes arranged in pyramids, his trays piled with cucumbers. Jack walked on, comfortable with the ordinariness of the people, their acceptance of him as their priest – for they knew who he was. It was he who would share their most precious life moments; their times of vulnerability and fear; their illnesses and death. He would be there.

He stepped into the darkened market hall where offal hung in ropes and slabs of meat, horns, skulls attached, waited on benches seething with flies. Women fingering purses stared concentratedly at the meat. Under the benches, like discarded gabardines, lay the insideout *carabao* skins, marked with traceries of pink veins. The air was intense. Shielding his eyes, he stepped back out into the bright daylight.

Child vendors squatting amongst piles of *choclos* and custard apples were playing five-stones; their shrieks of delight lost in the cry of men emptying shrimps, platter by platter into buckets, sloshing water, shouting. The secrets of these families would be laid bare before him in the confessional... his people, given to him, their concerns his concerns; their welfare, his welfare; their happiness, his. He stepped back to let a bicycle laden with chicken crates pass. They knew what a priest was. And he was theirs.

Returning home, Victor removed his boots.

"Telephone call for you!" Efigenia called.

"I'll take it in the study."

Ernesto came on the line.

"There *is* something going on."

"Not here."

"Golf club. 20 minutes."

Efigenia looked up: "Are you going out?" He kissed the top of her head. "What is it?"

"Nothing for you to worry about."

"But lunch?"

"Don't worry."

He drove carefully. Was anything ever secure? He'd been lucky in the banana, a *grass* not a tree, needing little attention. When it finished fruiting it collapsed and a new one took its place without the need to sow, thin or replant. He had made great savings with the cableway. One day machines would rip up the entire plant, hang it on the cableway, bring it to the sheds and shake off and pack the bananas by gravity or some other force. Humans would go, yes, and their expense. In the same way as the cableway had paid for its own construction in terms of labour saved, this would happen – given Time and the careful management of finances.

He found Ernesto at the bar.

"We'll go outside."

The men ambled to Ernesto's pickup.

"There *are* meetings in Manila. The doormen, the taxis, the room service – all confirm -"

"Where are they coming from?"

"Foreign."

"Of course foreign! You didn't pay for *that* did you? Where?"

"*Transnational* has no country."

"Private money or UN pledged?"

Ernesto shook his head. "This is back talk. The meetings weren't in conference rooms. They were at congressmen's houses…"

"Which congressmen?"

Ernesto shook his head.

"For God's sake that is *key!* How do we know which area is being affected without knowing the congressmen?"

"Look." Ernesto was annoyed. "You're turning into an old hen! There is *always* development going on." He pulled a map from his dashboard. "Look!" It was the standard motoring map with the islands of the Philippines laid out like sausages, a large one at each end and a handful of varying sizes in the middle. Victor noticed the spurious "proposed highway" joining them all, its spurious "tunnels" and "bridges" all pencilled in and the word 'feasibility' scrawled to one side.

"Here!" Ernesto smacked Luzon, the largest island at the very opposite end from Mindanao.

"It's as likely to be up there!" He smacked the far tip, a mountainous area.

"Your fingers are almost off the map! It could be here!"

"Why does everything have to be Mindanao with you? Up there -" he smacked the map again, "There's been a major struggle going on for, what, *5 years?* – to shift the Ifugao tribes – thousands of them – from those valleys so's they can flood and dam them up to make electricity for the lowlands, for Manila. *Massive* project. I think you can see, Victor, even you, that Manila is more important than Davao City! Put Mindanao from your mind!"

"So why is it taking so long?"

"Because the New Peoples Army, the NPA to you, drummed armed resistance into the local population who refused to leave their ancestral lands. Thanks to NPA stroke Church efforts at getting word out," he slammed the map shut, "the international press got hold of it so it's on off on off."

"If *that* project's gone cold - "

"That will never happen." Ernesto leaned across, pulled open the dashboard, showering Victor's knees with old cigarette lighters. "Your single event – one family – will be someone with a bit of pull, allowing his goons to let off steam." He shoved the map back in the dashboard, slammed it shut. "Let's eat."

Victor drove home. How well did he know Ernesto? The man had been able to pencil in the exact locations of the spurious tunnels and bridges... He tried to cheer himself. The Americans would protect him. When they'd come looking for a grower, he'd been their man, met their terms. When they'd asked that he discard all bananas below or above a certain length, wicked though the waste was, he'd complied. When they'd sent men to 'experiment' with banana lengths, make little finger bananas or the extra-large Cavendish – he'd taken them seriously and insisted Efigenia do the same. These men were Gods. They controlled copra, pineapple, sugar, palm oil, tuna…. When world prices weren't to their liking they let commodities slump. So far, thank God, bananas had held up. He checked left and right, swinging onto the tarmac road. Other growers had come unstuck trying to export to closed markets, signing agreements without expert guidance. They'd gone for copra – hopeless; rubber, easily manipulated; sugar even – which had taken everything from the soil and was now doomed because of sucrose. He took the turning on to his land. He knew things because the Americans told him. They supplied Japan on his behalf. They looked out for him. Mindanao was green, rich, frontier territory – and he didn't intend to make any mistakes.

He revved the vehicle. If God played right by him, he'd play right by God. The school, the bus service, the clinic, the netball team *belonging to his Estate* - the "Miss Cavendish" competition – movies would come once a month…

Reaching home he was tense and tired. Efigenia read the signs.

"We're going to the beach this afternoon. All of us." She fussed around him. "You work too hard."

"Victoria Beach?"

"Too far. Just the foot of our cliff."

The cliff let down in a jumble of wild vines and foliage onto a narrow strip of brilliant white sand met by a sea so clear that lines of sea anemones could be detected, blue and purple, in dips which were first to fill when the tide came in. It was not good swimming because of jellyfish which trailed long tentacles that left crimson whip marks and so intense a pain the shock could cause drowning. It was quiet now, the water the colour of foreigner's eyes, that peculiar unreasoning blue that frightened Efigenia. Further out it became dark, tinted with mauve, betraying a deep reef rich in shells which occasionally surfaced in the market.

Efigenia began setting up chairs.

"I'll do that -."

Sinking into one she watched Victor move about in his Bermuda shorts.

He looked middle aged: running to fat. He would not allow Ricky or Fredo to help with the barbecue. Never did, but what a blessing they got on, her men! So different! Ricky almost ready to step into his father's shoes; Fredo, squeamish at the very thought of pigs going to the abattoir – yet very good at running it off hog manure and tater, whatever that was, mixed in a 'digester' …Here they all were, except Norma, on an isolated beach with no sound but for Victor chinking the equipment. No radios or smells of lotions. Just the slap of the sea.

She looked at the maids: Loretta, Angela and Ninette mingling with her younger children; and beyond them, Jorge and Guinaldo, starting secondary school and allowed to have matches, setting fire to the dead leaves of a giant breadfruit tree, enjoying the crackle. Suddenly a large blue crab shot out.

Her eyes closed then opened again on shouts as Ninette and the littlest children ran amongst fallen caper flowers, poking fingers into the silky stamens, running to throw them in the sea or carry them back to the tree so the ants could crawl out and resume their journeys. On his own little Benjie amassed mallow flowers in pink tinged wreaths at her feet, the blooms' black spots blinking up at her. Her eyes closed.

The smell of the lobster drifted across. She opened her eyes. They had been through a lot together, she and Victor, since the day they had married. First that two roomed house in Quiapo: she 18, he 20 – going out each day, losing himself in the city, trying to find a way up. That little house, with its view of the home for unwanted children. It had been only a stone's throw from the cemetery where the cholera victims were buried.

She watched Ricky and Fredo disappear towards the next loop of beach, separated from theirs by a small hill jutting into the water... Once that hill had been a promontory but successive tides had cut it off, turned it into a small island from which trees leant at angles over the sea. The bay beyond housed a fishing community, its beach littered with dug-outs, patched sails and giant shells from which they had scooped the occupants.

She glanced across at Victor. The sky was losing its light, becoming yellow. By now the children were collecting tree pods, using them as bats to send round seeds flying.

The tide was low. Two distant urchins could be seen following each other along the sea's edge, baskets on their hips, occasionally stooping to swish water over them. They were *Badjaos,* sea gypsies from Zamboanga who had become Christian and been forced to settle on land away from their own area. Ricky had said that from the top of the hill their cemetery could be seen, its crude crosses poking between *Cabbage Palms,* overcome by *Strangler Figs.* Their village, he'd said was built on stilts over sand instead of water, only a band of windswept palms separating it from the brilliant sea.

Efigenia cracked the lobster. The evening was perfect. Except when the wind changed and the smell of mangrove mud drifted around from the estuary. She tossed a broken claw into the foliage. A night heron moved briskly away.

Standing in half light, Norma paused on the cliff path watching the pelicans' short ungainly bodies crash heavily into favoured spots in the mangroves, pull in, arrange their wings. She descended.

"So here you all are!"

"Norma! Some lobster -"

Efigenia watched her hold the lobster and stare across the bay, focussing on a scattering of lights blinking on a beach.

Victor glanced up. Fredo and Ricky were joshing the children sitting round Efigenia's feet, eating the bits she broke off. He stared. In a cotton shift, she looked like any market woman: her stomach bulged, her arms were heavy, her thighs thick. But as she picked thorns from her children's feet, got up, folded chairs or smacked mosquitoes on her arms, he sensed the wonder of her. From the slender beauty he had felt privileged to touch had come this encompassing woman. And together they had left childhood behind.

"Time to pack up." Efigenia announced.

The children were circling, pointing at bats, flashing against the lime green sky.

They climbed the cliff path together, hands linked.

Back at the house, Ricky drew him aside.

"I'd like to do something. Next week."

"You're a man now." Victor began walking away.

"I'll need the vehicles!"
But Victor kept going. Ricky frowned. Had his father lost his stomach for action?

Feeling deeply uneasy Victor drove to the plantation and sat on a bench outside the packing shed where workers on overtime were busy. Children stopped to stare. Leaning against the shed he listened to guitar notes filtering through the banana groves, smelt pork cooking. Never had Efigenia seemed more beautiful than when she was ushering their children up the cliff path. He watched an old man come out of the plantation store clutching a bottle of cooking oil. He looked both ways, crossed the path and vanished in the direction of the single men's quarters. Victor knew him. Twice widowed. He'd met his second wife there in the packing shed before the refrigeration plant opened. A young girl came out of the store with a clove of garlic. Rice, sugar, cooking oil, even cigarettes were subsidised and cheaper here than in town.

The young girl walked towards the married quarters. In town she would have been vulnerable but accommodation on the plantation was free: it stopped people putting up shacks, kept them in one area, and saved them money as did the supply of drinking water which kept them healthy.

"Do you like it here?" he called to her as she passed.
"Yes Sir. I will stay as long as the company wants me."
Let Ricky think he was getting old: he had done good. Yet the feeling lingered ....

In the bedroom that night he knelt and said his prayers: "You know God that I want to do this thing for you and for Efigenia. But she doesn't understand about spare capital. If its spare, it isn't capital. I *need* to keep that vacant lot for Jorge… maybe Guinaldo can go into machinery repair if the cardboard box factory doesn't work out – if he shows aptitude. The girls will marry. I can't sell off Fredo's piggery. It's the one thing that really works! One minute a head for full slaughter; fifteen minutes to skin a cow! And what about Benjie? … The point, God …" He looked up at Efigenia, already in bed, hair pinned in place, reading. "Please show me how to do this. She wants her hospital -" He dipped his head. "Hospitals cost. Another thing, I'm worried that something might be going on down here. I don't know who to trust. Please guide me." He paused. "In the past I may have failed to please but I'm doing my best now." He got into bed.

Efigenia had a mischievous look on her face: "You know, what would be pleasing to God Victor -" she tickled his chin: "If you're so short of cash, why don't you sell your race horse!"

Chapter 5

First thing in the morning Victor got moving.

"I'm seeing the bank manager this afternoon. I want you to invite the people on this list to dinner next Thursday. Formal dinner."

Efigenia scanned the list.

"We are pushing the boat out!"

"Good food. Plenty of it."

"What is the occasion?"

"All in good time, my dear."

"I shall see some of them at church on Sunday -"

"Formal written invitations. To arrive Monday."

Today would be a Friday like no other.

Norma headed into town. She was bored. Things had stopped happening because since the 'incident' at Hotel Davao the chain had been broken. Which meant Mindanao had gone silent and the NPA and the world would think things were fine. So what kind of an 'operative' was she to allow this to happen? Too afraid to be NPA herself, yet she would dearly have loved to meet one. Sometimes she dreamt of them: young men who'd given up everything, lived hard lives…Brave, tough …And women too. Would they admire *her*? Yes, she took risks, lead a double life … There *was* a slim chance that she might be killed but for them, death was a reality. They'd abandoned their student lives. Even if they survived, they could never return to Society. Year on year hiding and running, trying to educate peasants in their rights, to bring them care, hygiene, *marrying them* even – sharing their uncomfortable lives. If she could *meet* one! But she wouldn't know one if she met him. Because no one would identify them. *Who was it* that had gathered information and deposited it at Hotel Davao? Was it one person? Two? She stopped her car to think. The chain was broken because the person who had gathered the information and deposited it at the Hotel Davao was missing. That person had been known to Brother Tomas. Or at least there had been a sign or he wouldn't have been able to indicate whether the information had got through safely: he couldn't have nodded or shaken his head at her or Alicia those times. Was *he* the link? Unlikely. Did *he* pass information to a second link who carried it to Hotel Davao, or was his role simply to pass the signal? He was worth trying. Because of torture, people were careful not to know more than their immediate attachment. She and Alicia had accepted tape recordings, typed them up, slipped the paper copy to a mild looking student who volunteered at the beach office of SCAPS (The Share and Care Apostolate for Poor Settlers). *His* associates would not have known about her and Alicia. And he would only have known that either she or Alicia delivered the material: nothing more.

Contact had to be re-established – the link put back so the chain could function. Without Alicia it was up to her. But carefully. She must test possibilities without exposing herself; listen for the nuance in a voice, seek the wavering in an eye which, after much fencing, said: "I know what you are and you know what I am and we know that we know." So start with Brother Tomas! She reversed and set off driving cautiously along a minor road. Confidently she turned into the entrance of the Lodge where the native clergy lived, got out, rang the bell.

A priest appeared.

"Miss Salcedo!"

"Brother Tomas please. I have a Mass request."

He ushered her into a parlour. After a considerable wait Brother Tomas appeared, looking drawn. No need to bother with *I happened to be passing:* he would prefer not to know. But his discomfort suggested he knew.

"Would you have any objection," Norma began, seeking his eyes, finding them opaque, "if Father Jack," she continued, looking him very pointedly in the eye, "were to say the 10 o'clock Friday Mass – from now on?"

Brother Tomas' heart pounded. Had she been got at? She was too big to take out.

"He has difficulty with the early Mass on Fridays," she continued looking at him steadily.

"As a permanent arrangement?" he asked, his eyes little points.

"Yes." She looked him hard in the eye.

"*Are you – sure –*" he glanced from side to side " – he would be prepared – to - do this?"

She saw his toes tighten in his sandals.

"If you think -" she drew breath – "the arrangement – could be made to work –"

He looked down. Oh God, let this not be a trap. He looked up. Her eyes flickered. *She was afraid. The girl was afraid.* He rummaged in his pocket, pulled out a small gold key.

"He'll need a duplicate of this. It will be sufficient for him to leave mine under the altar cloth –" He stared at Norma. "He should on no account give it to -" he paused "anyone else."

Norma looked blank. Was he implicating the sacristan?

"Thank you." She pocketed the key. He opened the door but did not watch her leave. The sheer unlikeliness of the girl made her safe…. Fear sliding off him he heard her car turn and speed off.

Jack waited patiently until Josie, the woman who 'did for him' had gone. He had no idea who paid her, but she arrived every morning at 7.00 and as far as he could make out, her day consisted of coffee, market, washing, bed making, a good look in the cupboards, cleaning, lunch, siesta (listening to a tiny transistor radio), ironing, the evening meal, the dishes and goodnight. The daily highlight was pudding: usually a slice of fruit about to go off – not that food was very important to him. Just as well as it was served stone cold to conserve charcoal, the lunchtime beans and potatoes being boiled at the same time as the paraffiny tasting morning coffee was brewed in whatever heat could be drawn from the cooling charcoal. Enough water was boiled in the morning for a thermos for their afternoon tea but as the lid fitted poorly, despite her time spent re-wrapping shreds of cloth around the cork, the water hardly stayed hot. At least he was living like the people. Yesterday's main meal, always midday, had consisted, apart from watery soup, of a plate of penny sized red crabs, shells and all, which Josie was clearly very proud to have obtained. She had stood watching him maternally from the doorway, then come and sat shyly opposite him to "show him how", throwing them sideways into her mouth, smiling encouragement and crunching loudly. The fridge, an item she felt had no place in a kitchen, contained nothing but a Johnny Walker bottle of tap water. There was nothing in the cupboard under the sink. No tins, bottles, dishwashing liquids... The sink – he was beginning to recognise it as a typical Filipino sink – had one cold tap, an untangled scouring pad with rice and vegetable matter caught up in it. What food he hadn't eaten waited between plates on top of the fridge for Josie to take home in the evening.

Hunting for a biscuit, Jack heard the kitchen door opening and footsteps coming through. Norma entered, quickly switched off the room lights, closed the shutters, put the lights back on.

"What are you doing?"

"Better for you if no one sees me here "

She sat opposite him.

"I'm going to trust you. That may not be a good idea – "

"Thank you. "

"You're – how can I say – you don't understand things that most people here take for granted -"

"Yet people don't treat me like an imbecile –"

"Refuse if you want – but swear – swear to God you will keep this quiet –" Her eyes were serious. "You mustn't tell anyone. Not my mother. Not a friend. Not another priest. No one. Do you agree?"

"You can trust me Norma –"

She produced the key.

"I had this cut for you. I think it's the tabernacle."

"No –" Jack picked it up. "The tabernacle key is larger. It hangs in the Vestry wardrobe. Anyone can get it. Eucharistic ministers, visiting priests. The Sacristan shows them."

"Then what is it the key to?"

"Where did you get it?"

"I can't say."

Jack turned it over in his hands and thought his way round the Cathedral.

"It'll be – a small tabernacle – one of the side altars. Didn't think they were used." Norma nodded. "What do I do with it?"

"Look inside. I'll wait here. Use a torch. Don't put the lights on."

Jack stood. "I may be some time!"

Norma sat listening to insects, watching a gecko on the ceiling. Finally she heard steps. She jumped up.

"Eureka!" Jack placed an envelope on the table. Norma opened it. Scraps of paper fluttered across the table. Norma unfurled the first one, passed it to Jack. He read.

"Dear God!"

She flattened several on the table.

"Fr. Frank, the American priest, was salvaged for these." She indicated the notes.

"Salvaged?"

"Killed and dumped. About the time you arrived."

"How do you know?"

"It was in the Detainee Situationer. That's a monthly sheet of – 'events' – like these," she smacked the pile of notes.

"This defies belief!"

"This is not a game you can withdraw from. You could be killed. Being a priest will not protect you. Though to some extent my father will."

"What do you want me to do?"

"To collate the notes, put them on tape. For every death, every disappearance - there is a witness. There is an information network like underground water. If there are obstacles, it flows around them. Some people get wasted but – if you care about people like that woman Emerenciana -"

"Emma who?"

"The woman in the bloodstained dress who came to our house when you first arrived: she turned up at that beach I showed you."

Jack picked up the notes: "You want me to put them on a tape for you to type? I don't have a tape recorder. Can you get me one?"

"I daren't be seen buying one."

"Where will I find these notes?"

"You will find them."

"What if there are none?"

"Do nothing."

"Perhaps they will be in the side tabernacle again –"

"They won't. Because you will have the key. Protect it with your life. Or more accurately, protect your life with it. Was there a cloth on that altar?"

"Yes."

"Slip this other key under it. I don't want to know which one it was." She passed him the key. The room was still.

"Why do you take such chances Norma?"

"A purpose. I need one. Same as you. In some countries protesting women cut their hair like men or march for gay rights. Here that would be pointless and dangerous. To succeed here you must be invisible so I must be like all Filipino girls. They have long hair and taunt men to the point they almost need to be raped. But make no mistake – they do it from behind a very high fence they have no intention of crossing."

"Maybe – just maybe –" Jack began. "You know I'm learning *Tagalog?* If I could buy a <u>Teach Yourself Tagalog</u> course and tape machine –"

"Hah! You can't even buy university text books down here! You certainly won't find that kind of thing!"

"If I had a machine, my teacher could put phrases on tape for me to practice – "

Norma grasped Jack's wrist. "That's a very good idea!"

"For pronunciation."

"Of course! Suggest it to the Sacristan! Let him think it's his idea. Offer to pay him if he can find a machine. He'll certainly find one because he can overcharge you! That is how things work here! But practice loudly at odd hours so nothing is thought of it. Because you will be spied on."

"And I give you the tapes?"

"Once a week. My mother will invite you to eat at our house."

"I find the whole thing incredible."

"That is why you could be useful."

"As long as it doesn't clash with my priestly vows – "

"If someone puts a note or something for you to publicly 'find' – ignore it. Say 'Is this yours?' Flick it in the bin. Never ask questions. Later, if you take it out to copy, put it back in the bin. But don't ask questions."

"But if it's a set up – and I repeat it - and it ends up in your Detainee Situationer –"

"If you do it properly, by the time it's out – no one will know who repeated it. You left it in a public bin, remember?"

"What if someone like that woman who came to your house comes to me for help?"

80

"Tell her the truth. You are a foreign priest. You don't understand. It's shocking."

"But –"

"Let them ask around. Someone else will tell them. You know nothing. You believe there are refugees at a beach somewhere. That's common knowledge." Norma glanced at the door. "I won't be able to see so much of you now." She rose, hesitated, moved to the door – with something unsaid. She left. A sadness settled on Jack.

Efigenia had waited up. She caught the look in Norma's eyes as she entered. "You're late."

Norma shrugged. Was there a man in this Efigenia wondered? Norma was at a dangerous age.

"Now that you are developing social graces perhaps you would think about marriage?"

Norma looked distant.

"At least give some thought to sort of man you could be attracted to - "

Norma shook her head.

"Then we'll set about finding one for you."

"I'm not marrying."

"You may dislike the *fact* of your womanhood –"

"I don't dislike it."

"What do you want that marriage can't provide?"

"Something unspeakably vulgar."

Morning. Norma walked on the beach to the sound of the wind. That had been an unkind thing to say to her mother. She'd better say sorry. True though: not that the woman would know it. Vulgar. *Vulgaris.* Latin. Of the people. Popular. Social Justice. That was what she wanted. But no one could stand up and use those words without

81

getting killed, or at the very least interrogated. And what use was she anyway? She had given nothing up. She was still Norma Salcedo, with her bed, her food, her future. She *might* end up mutilated in some filthy bathroom like Alicia. Perhaps that would happen to the English priest too. Why was everything such a struggle? *Is* it my moral duty to struggle, she wondered? But how could she know what she knew and not resist it? Every day it was happening.

If the English priest saw a picture in the paper of Imelda Marcos in front of half built houses handing out title deeds to grateful workers who had been relocated from Manila: if he read that a cigarette factory was being established near the site especially for them as it was too far for them to return to their old jobs now that their original homes had gone, would he still think 'how nice'? Would he guess that the day after the cameras stopped rolling, the title deeds would be taken back? *That* was common knowledge! If he were told that the rent for the unfinished shells was 400 pesos a month, exactly a full month's wage at the cigarette factory, would it make him sit up? Would he believe, even if he were told, that nobody got that wage anyway because the factory laid off workers every six months in order to pay them the lower piece rate…? Every Filipino seeing those photos in the papers knew the people would end up in roadside shacks while the developers finished the houses and sold them to wealthy buyers! She kicked a fishing float. How could this be stopped? She sat on the wet sand, looking at the sea. People took refuge in religion. She snapped a twig. Greed understood armed resistance. Not words. Here at the beach, the people SCAPS counselled had given up their *rights* to existence. They were *wasted*. Finding herself turning over a stone in her hand she flung it at the sea. Cooperation didn't work. *Fighting* was needed. And here was she, a white-collar revolutionary, doing paperwork. Armed resistance: that was what developers understood. Backed by international publicity with common ordinary people around the world standing up and shaming the multinational developers, their shareholders and investors. Yet what she was doing was being done by nobody else. That had to mean something. So why did she want to be big and famous? Surely to be another piece of grass in the lawn should be enough?

During Sunday Mass Jack was conscious of the Salcedos in the front row beaming proudly at him. All 10 of them. A great fuss of him was made at the door.

"How are you settling in Father! Is that housekeeper giving you fish soup and rice for breakfast? I've offered her eggs. Look Victor, Father is wasting away to skin and bone! Come to dinner with us Father -"

"I'm fine!"

"Father, this is a Special Mass Intention –." Victor pressed an envelope into his hands. Jack glimpsed concern in his eyes. "The offering is inside -"

"You don't need to make an offering. I always include your family in my prayers."

"It's our pleasure."

"Good morning Father"

"Good morning Father"

People flowed past.

"You must buy meat! Protein! You are a young man!" Efigenia continued. "Feed your body!"

"Excuse me – " Jack turned to arrange a baptism for a couple, radiant with their infant.

"Father –" Efigenia pressed. "We are having a dinner party next Thursday. Do please come. Say you will!"

Jack beamed. "That sounds seriously good! I'd love to – "

"And stay the night! We've missed you, haven't we Victor!?"

Beyond them Jack glimpsed Norma in a group of the young, well heeled, dressed to the nines, leaning against her car, one leg slightly raised, head on one side, hair falling. Her laugh rang out, fresh, attractive, vivacious; socialising at church like young people everywhere.

"See you in a minute!" she called to her parents, not once looking at Jack.

"Victor," Efigenia took his arm. "What is the Special Intention?"

"There are always things to pray for."

"Is everything alright?"

"Of course." He patted her arm. "How else are we to give the boy money?"

"The *priest,* Victor."

Secretly Jack was looking forward to staying at Mansion Salcedo. He carefully packed a bag, purchased a gift for Efigenia and arrived by cab.

"Father Jack!" Efigenia exclaimed. "Out of the kitchen! Angela! Fetch Father a cold beer."

Norma watched Efigenia pour the beer, watched Jack's eyes lighting up at the sounds and smells from the kitchen.

"We have extra help in," Efigenia explained.

"If you like while we wait I can show you the cliff path –" Norma said boredly.

"After his beer Norma. Let Father finish his beer."
Unlatching the screen door, Norma stepped out. Jack
followed, drinking his beer, trying to look interestedly at
black stains running down the house walls, vines growing
from cracks in the plaster, a *papaya* tree springing from a
balustrade.

"Hurry up with your beer."

"Stand still. Your mother's watching."

Savouring the beer, Jack looked around.   Where an
English family would have created a place 'to be together
outside', here was just 'the back': where servants sat by a
washing line draped across trodden earth and *frangipani*
blossoms lay on blackened automobile parts. An escaped
bougainvillea had scrambled over a well with a bent pipe
coming from it. There was no attempt at extending the
idea of civilisation into the wilderness. No colonisation!

"Ready."

Jack passed the bottle back through the screen door,
ducked under the frangipani trees, following Norma past
the well.

"Have you got the tape?"

"Yes."

"Wait 'til we get away from the house." Her skirt
caught a tapioca shrub. "You might as well have a look at
the view while you're here." She pointed ahead. "This is
the Gulf of Davao.   On the left – *Davao Oriental,* that
narrow finger of land. Over there Davao del Sur goes on
and on. And back of it –" She glanced around. "We're
OK now."

Jack handed Norma the tape. She pushed it inside her
blouse.

"How did you get rid of the notes?"

"In a bin."

"Where?"

"On the street."

"!For God's sake! The homemade sweet seller'll wrap sweets in them; the larger ones'll go for twists of peanuts; some urchin'll sell the big ones to a public toilet! Tell the world, why don't you!?"

"Sorry."

"Did anyone see?"

"I hope not."

"Someone always sees everything."

"I thought you wanted the information known."

"Not that way! The Government doesn't *want* people collecting information because people aren't supposed to have disappeared! If your name gets tied to this –"

"I'll be more careful –"

"You'd better be. Especially at supper tonight. You don't know what's going on –"

A chiming reached them.

"That's the gong."

They entered the crowded room separately.

"Everybody! Everybody! This is Father Jack!"

Women in bright colours, winged sleeves disguising the curves of age, looked up, smiled and turned back to each other, exchanging pleasantries across their husbands.

"Did you meet the Mayor yet," Efigenia placed her hand at Jack's elbow, steering him towards a large man at the table's end. "He lost the election," she whispered. "But Victor had him re-instated."

Chairs scraped back as the men stood, Victor resplendent in hand-worked silk shirt. "We like to dress up!" Victor nudged Jack conspiratorially. "Please sit next to me!"

"What is the occasion?"

Efigenia winked. "You'll see." She tapped her silverware on a glass: "Everybody! Father Jack will say Grace!"

During the meal the table talk, led by the women, was of family – many of whom were present – of amusing incidents with domestics, of sad events like the death of a child, of weddings and engagements.

"Victor is rather hoping you will make a speech later," Efigenia whispered to Jack. "Supporting his project. Word has already got out –"

"Which project is this?"

"How much it will cost?" Guinaldo asked.

"Not at table!"

"I was saying," Efigenia turned to the matron next to her.

"How nice it is to have Father Jack amongst us." The matron looked at Jack blankly.

"The further I get from the seminary, the less use I seem to be!" Jack demurred.

"It's a big vocation. You don't fall into it like – like -"

"A banana baron?"

"Thank you Norma."

"An automobile salesman," Efigenia corrected. "People who achieve, spend *years* …. We've been a bit naughty tonight and prepared your room. I do hope you'll stay?"

"Have you visited the needlework class on the plantation yet?" a woman asked.

"I'd love to."

"The American priests didn't. They were very educated," she said carefully. "But we didn't see much of them. They taught college -"

"You would see them having a beer in town like anyone else -" her husband put in.

"Not like priests at all really," the woman concluded.

"Hold it please -"

Ricky moved round the table with a camera. Victor leaned across and put an arm round Jack's shoulder: "Smile – Father -"

Used to being photographed, daughters in first off–the-shoulder dresses lent forward, tilting their heads and adolescent sons in cummerbunds and frills looked manfully at the camera. Finally the children were sent out to play.

"We can't wait any longer!" a wife protested. "Out with it!"

Victor stood up.

"Those of you who know me well, know how close to my heart is the welfare of the people," he hesitated slightly. "That God has placed under me."

Jack sensed the men drawing back.

"What we have done in Mindanao, all of us -" his arm took in the influential men remaining at the table, "Is to further the interests not only of our Country – for which we can be proud – but to provide security to those not *able t*o negotiate with higher bodies."

The men watched warily.

"What I am proposing," Victor announced. "Offers not a penny's profit to anyone here. But, for those who wish to be associated with it, this is *one for God."*

The mayor leaned back in his chair.

"You all know I have long planned to build a sports facility. What, I ask you, is more important? Is it not a *hospital* for the people of this community?"

The political candidate glanced at the mayor.

Efigenia nudged Jack. He prepared to stand but with no idea what to say. Victor signalled 'not yet!'.

"There is room for all who wish to be part of this project," Victor smiled at the wives. "Who wish to be remembered – *one way or another* -"

Like pigeons on crumbs the women fell on their husbands.

"Why didn't we think of it?"

"We must support this!"

"Bless you!" A matron squeezed Efigenia's hand.

"We owe it to Father Jack's good influence," Efigenia demurred. "And the night before Victor saw the bank manager about it," she blushed. "I stayed up saying the rosary!"

"It's paid for then?" A man said loudly.

"Could our maids use it?" his wife interrupted. "Will it be attached to the plantation?"

"Is it paid for?" the man repeated.

"Who is *he?*" Jack whispered to Norma.

"Cement," Norma muttered.

"The point *is*," Efigenia told her neighbours. "If *we* don't do it, who will?"

Cement banged his glass on the table: "So you want 'support'. In cash?"

Once the ladies had withdrawn, the serious fencing began.

"Like I said," Victor began. "The money is in place. With a shortfall. But I'll need someone to open the building -"

"A job for the mayor -"

"*Which* mayor?" The political candidate demanded. "I would have thought, given that the KBL party represents this area -"

"Friends, friends," Victor interrupted. "There will be room for everyone's name above the door!" He smiled around. "Or, more importantly, should I say, their *wives.*"

Jack stepped out onto the balcony.

"I can't *stand* those people," Norma said, glaring back at the men through their cigar smoke. "Look at them, jockeying!"

"They're well intentioned -"

"Are they? Don't you know what you're seeing? You were only invited so my father could get a photo of The Church supporting his project. Tomorrow morning's press headlines will be: CHURCH BACKS HOSPITAL DEVELOPMENT. You'll see. Don't you mind being used?"

"Not as long as the food is good."

"You don't mean that."

"No.   But maybe not all people fit into this sociopolitical framework you have constructed.   Isn't it just possible that some rich people are decent?"

"Pathetic."

"Alright. Pathetic but decent."

"The pathetic is *you!*"

Long after the last car had left, unable to sleep, Jack rose and crossed to the window. His old room felt different.   Yet, the evening had made him aware how at home he felt with the Salcedos and that, despite her prickliness, Norma was the closest he'd come to having a friend. He glanced onto the drive, then stood, not believing his eyes. Three of Salcedo's S.D.C.I. pickups, cloths pasted over the motifs on their doors, were being pushed silently down the drive, on their backs armed

90

men. Gently closing the shed door, a man ran after the last pickup, jumped in the back and leaned forward, grabbing a machine gun. The last to climb on was Ricky. As the vehicles reached the road, Jack could just make out the sound of engines starting up.

"There is one thing I must ask," Jack said as Victor prepared to drive him back to the Cathedral next morning.
"What were those trucks I saw leaving your place with armed men last night?"
Victor did not hesitate. "The C.H.D.F. The Civil Home Defence Force. You'll have read about them in the paper. President Marcos gave responsible persons permission to form local defence groups -"
   "Quasi-military?"
   "Yes. Some probably even serve on your altar. I have all their names. I armed them. They have to return the arms each time."
   "What is their purpose?"
   "To prevent such kinds of incident as befell that unfortunate woman who visited us soon after you arrived. Remember? Army units trespassing on homesteads, thugs…"
Jack nodded, recalling the tape he had dictated.
   "The men you saw are unpaid volunteers. We patrol when we are not expected. Like last night. Or if there are reports of intruders in the area." He started the pickup.
   "It's a sad situation to have to patrol your own country, I admit." The vehicle purred along. "I'm sorry we woke you. We try to be quiet but with untrained men… doors get slammed." He clapped Jack on the shoulder. "Efigenia has some stuff for you." He thumbed a portable

two-burner camp stove and butane bomb in the back. "Show that housekeeper how to use it and don't let her skimp. The butane man will call once a week. The bill's taken care of."

"That is really kind of you -"

"Things are looking good for me. I thank God for it."

"I hope you don't think -"

"We have to watch out for so-called rebels in Mindanao too," Victor paused before turning onto the main road. "They are no different from any other thug except they pretend a philosophy." He waited while a lizard ran from the grass and crossed the road. "People just want to get on with their lives." He checked both ways. "If they have a genuine case, I subscribe to that. But if they're carpetbaggers, they can watch out!"

Chapter Six

It was a week since the party. Victor plunged his arm into the tank used for rinsing off bananas. Too bad if chemicals floated there: he could not go home to Efigenia with red dust, grit on his arms. He turned the hose on the pickup watching the earth run in swathes down it's metal sides to fall on the ground. He spread it with one foot. It was a different colour from the plantation earth.

Dawn was coming up. Time to be gone. The sheaves of his banana plantation glistened lemon yellow. A bird called. Soon humans would begin moving about, worn thongs tripping on fallen trunks, hands pushing spiders' webs aside as they hurried to where they had left off the previous day. He climbed quietly into the pickup. By 7 o'clock the place would echo with the sound of voices, with loud mechanical clanking, as the hundreds of green bananas, limped by wire and pylon over pulleys to their destiny.

The pickup's wheels gripped the metalled road. So that was what Ricky had been up to! He touched the stubble on his chin. There was always the odd family who dug in and insisted that because they had *been there* a number of years they had *rights*. If they'd had rights, they would've had *title* and Government didn't give title to common squatters who'd be sitting on small plots amid valuable land when developers came along; who could not 'pay': who would want 'compensation'. It was the lawyers who were wrong for taking on such cases, for encouraging people to think they had rights. At least with *him* people knew where they stood. *He* did things the right way, kept the ruling KBL candidate in office, made sure the Mayor was 'correctly disposed' on national issues. He'd been awarded a Medal of Appreciation from the President and when the American priests had written letters which appeared in the American press and embarrassed Manila, he'd moved swiftly to get them out! Still, nonetheless …. He stopped the vehicle, bit at his thumb. Don't think about it.

He wound down the window, rested an elbow there. The local press had not missed his bid for a hospital. That was good. He drove along, the thought of the settlers scrambling like chickens bothering him. He recalled the first time Ricky had wanted land and remembered himself, somewhat righteously, saying: "You do know there are people there, don't you?" Ricky had looked him straight in the eye. "Yes," he'd said. A plea for equality, for partnership. For recognition. And proud of his son, he'd replied: "Move them. You know how."

As the familiar palms of Mansion Salcedo appeared at the top of the hill, he overcame it. You could not tell a man how to do his job – especially in the matter of women. Some of them were killers many times over; killed for the joy. It was their sin. They were not asked to commit it. Controlling his own men was Ricky's business and he must forget the matter. By now Ricky had probably seen their lawyer, put in the land claim truthfully stating: "None" in the box for "Present Occupiers". It was not as if … he threw the keys on a ledge. *At least he was building a hospital.*

Entering the house he found Efigenia on a step-ladder removing a picture of the Sacred Heart and handing it to Loretta.

"Oh thank goodness you're here! Quick. Pass up the picture of President Marcos."

"What are you doing?"

"Where *were* you?"

"I had something to check on -"

"Did you come to bed last night? Here!" Loretta handed up the picture. "The Americans phoned. A Mr. Garvay and Mr. Coloman."

"*Colman.*"

"They wrote a week ago -"

"From America?"

"They're at the Century Park Sheraton! They'll be at the airport by now -"

"The Century Park Manila?"

"Yes! If you'd been here at breakfast -"

Efigenia stumbled backwards off the ladder. Loretta caught her.

"How did they sound?"

"As usual." She slammed the ladder shut. "Very rude."

Victor nodded. His wife did not like their concentration on business to the exclusion of family.

"Did they say why they were coming?"

"To me? They want to talk to you. Loretta, go upstairs and see how their rooms are coming on. I sent Fredo to the airport to get them."

"Why not Ricky?"

"Can't find him."

"You're coping wonderfully." He caressed her head. No point letting the woman get in a state. She relaxed at once.

"I try Victor, but they are somehow so - *inhuman*. Not Americans. I love their childish informality. Your *business friends.*"

"Tunnel vision."

"And this isn't much notice."

"Our deliveries have been perfect. Our payments are up to date. I guarantee no one has found a single worm in a Salcedo banana."

"It won't be a social visit."

"The shortage of hotels forces them to stay privately. They may have other projects down here."

"*Now* what are you doing?"

"I have time for a bath, surely?"

Efigenia picked at her hair.

"If it was serious we would have heard," Victor reassured her.

"I've sent Manuel to bring the children home early from school."

"Whatever for?"

"As a – a – *charm* against their rudeness."

Efigenia could see it wasn't working. She had clustered the children, all dressed like little men and women – in the entranceway, where they were enthusiastically singing an American song, accompanied by Ricky on the guitar.

"Today while the blossom

Still clings to the vine

We'll eat your strawberries

And drink your sweet wine

A million tomorrows

May all pass away

E'er we forget

All the joys

That are ours today."

Yet the men had walked straight past them into the lounge. Ushered by Ricky, the children had followed. Ricky had begun quickly to strum *"Mabuhay",* causing the children to burst into *Tagalog:*

"Da hilsa yo –"

"That means – 'Because of you –' Victor translated, handing out drinks. "*Mabuhay* – the word we use to welcome homecoming *balikpapan* -"
The Americans stood twisting their glass stems. Efigenia hushed the children. Norma clapped loudly, called: "Well done children!"
Embarrassed, Victor lit up a cigar. The Americans stepped out onto the balcony. Efigenia snatched the cigar.
"They don't like that!"
Victor stepped out onto the balcony.
Norma picked up their briefcase.
"What are you doing Norma?" demanded Efigenia.
"Just wondering if they're United, del Monte, Dole, Guthrie -"
"Put that case down!"
Victor slid open the balcony door: "Can you ask Ricky to join us? And don't disturb us for a while?"
"Bring out my case, why don't you Victor," called one of the men. "On second thoughts – you have an air-conditioned room we can use?"

Norma watched the Americans stepping past her mother, following her father into his study.

The door closed.

"Go and find Ricky."

"Do you think they'll eat here?"

"A finger buffet is coming. I've started on the meal -"

"What we want," Mr. Colman began. "Is for you to cease spraying pesticides."

Victor's face didn't change.

"Looking to the long term future – assuming you want to stay with us - " he waited. Victor's gaze was steady.

"There is concern about the soil. Our requirements are that instead of spraying bananas as they grow, you protect them within a man-sized polythene sheath. Any objections?" He looked up. "Up to now you've been spraying. We appreciate you rinse but fruits dipped in test chemicals in the home market come up with significant pesticide residue - "

"Nobody eats the skin."

Mr. Garvay turned to Ricky. "True. But we have the consumer lobby to contend with. Up until now 17% of the cost of each fruit has gone in pesticides and fertilizers. Am I right?"

Victor nodded.

"So this represents a saving for you."

"I wouldn't insult such an old friend," Victor said, trying to sound jovial. "By suggesting you came here to renegotiate our signed contracts on the price per crate on the basis of cheaper -"

"Not at all," Colman interrupted. "We're responding to the market. On your behalf. It's not clear what kind of fertilizer you use -"

"Local product."

Mr. Garvay riffled the papers.

"You don't state the chemical compounds. However there is additional concern that the long term run off from fertilizer will render soil infertile." He looked up wanting a reply.

"Not in our case."

"You and I both want to preserve what you have. Am I right? International land suitable for planting out is diminishing by the decade."

"On the face of it," Victor began but Colman interrupted.

"The world is running out of land Victor. Otherwise we wouldn't bother."

Efigenia put her head in: "May I bring in some snacks?"

"Applying shrouds is labour intensive," Victor was saying, his voice sounding a bit choked. Efigenia withdrew. "The workers will need supervision. That's a cut in profits. I have two aircraft for spraying -" He pulled himself up sharp. "But that's not a problem."

"You sure?"

"A reasonable consumer issue. Quite," Victor nodded. "Anything else?"

"One small thing, yes. There's interest in an experimental banana. Usual sort of exercise – Thought you might be the man for it -" Victor leaned forward but the words flowed over his head. More land. He'd need land…

"So what do you think Victor?"

"On the face of it, yes, it's a good idea. The consumer's right of course." He smiled affably. "Count me in."

Garvay passed over some sheets.

"No date is set for compliance with the polythene shrouds so the changeover period is up to you."

"Very generous."

"The payment per crate, you'll be glad to hear, remains the same." He allowed himself a smile. "Are you in agreement Victor?"

Victor eyed him steadily.

"What Mr. Colman is saying," Mr. Garvay interpreted. "Is that we are prepared *for a limited period of time* to accept a drop in production without invoking the penalty clause. How long do you think it will take you to change over?"

"I hope," Victor shrugged, " - to have the show on the road – as you say – by the end of this year. Say November."

"Congratulations! Good." The men rose, extending hands.

"It is such a pleasure to have you." Victor smiled automatically. "You will stay to dinner?"

Mr. Colman shook his head.

"We can make the afternoon flight."

"At least take a walk in the air. Manila cannot compete with that!"

The two men hesitated.

"Come! Five minutes then Ricky will drive you to the airport. Ricky - Go get the car!"

Ricky watched them leave the house. Was his father insane?

Bending to pick a burr from his pants leg, Garvay followed Victor and Colman across scrubland, sweat dripping from his forehead onto his shoes. "Ten minutes more." He told himself, following them into a darkened building. "Ten minutes more and we'll be away!"

Inside, the short Filipino was pointing at a horse reciting what sounded like Arabian names.

"Is that a fact," Colman was saying, his expression disguised by the darkness. Victor looked at his visitors' lanky legs, no doubt caused by breeding or environment:

"Do you ride perhaps? Go to the races, Mr. Colman?" He asked. "The sport of kings?"

Colman shook his head.

"Play polo?"

"Play what?"

"Polo. From the Tibetan word "*pulu*" meaning willow – the wood the balls were made from."

"You don't say."

"You didn't know that?"

If they were gentlemen they would have offered him compensation for the changeover, for the extra expense, for the cost of stockpiled pesticides.

"The Tibetans – thought to be *barbarians,*" Victor emphasized. "were playing polo 300 years before it reached the so-called *civilized* world."

Driving to the airport, radio on low, Ricky listened to their murmurs and grunts, catching, he thought, the words "took it well" and something that sounded like "horse! -" followed by a snicker.

At the airport he held their door open.

"We were pleased to have you here Sir. And you." He pumped their hands vigorously. The security guard stepped smartly aside. Picking up their briefcases, holding the military check back, Ricky escorted them across the tarmac, stood aside to let them mount the stairs, followed them onto the plane and seated them at the very front.

"Please come again Sirs. Remember that our home is your home!"

"Yeah ok." They were standing, their backs to him, pushing their attaché cases into the overhead lockers.

Stepping out of the men's room where he had looked at himself for a long time in the mirror, Ricky watched their plane circle and head off towards Manila. Bastards! And his father was losing it. Giving a changeover date they couldn't make. The fruits would ripen more slowly under plastic covers. OK they were shipped green and could outlast any number of industrial disputes but still they'd take longer to reach regulation packing size. What was he thinking of? He swerved out of the parking area. "We've had six inches of rain so far," he said aloud to the car. "Need at least eight. Rain doesn't begin again 'til November." Torn between hatred for the Americans and respect for their business acumen, he pressed the accelerator.

"What the hell are you playing at?" he demanded, bursting into Victor's study.

"Don't talk to me like that!" Victor snapped. "Just because you've had a kill."

"Are you trying to put us out of business?"

"You know nothing."

"That date is crazy!"

"If we haven't changed by then, we're dead anyway." He drummed fingers on his desk.

Ricky leant over him: "I disagree."

"How?"

"We continue spraying -"

"They'll test."

"- until the plastic sheaths arrive -"

"They won't take the current crop, so why bother?"

"They have to."

"They don't."

Ricky changed tack: "Why didn't you say this would put us in financial difficulties?"

"And have them go elsewhere? The company will *go on.* We must stay with it. The best we can hope for – we get the system up – but not running – by November."

"And plant beyond the deadline?"

"As I pushed for that deadline - " Victor shouted. "Against the other growers - to secure our dominance - that option is out!"

"Get the Decree waived!"

Victor shook his head. "We clear already planted land. Some of it. "The new plants'll take ten, eleven, months to mature fruit," he said slowly."They've waived supply. They've promised."

"Not for our sake."

The room became silent. Ricky broke it.

"You didn't handle it well."

Victor looked up "You know so much – tell me – what is our biggest problem?"

"The gap between the old system and the new -"

"Wrong!" Victor thumped the table. "Our main problem is the planes are not paid for."

"So?"

"And they are of no use to us -"

"Sell them!"

"To whom? Bauzon would've known this was coming when he mounted that special on aviation fuel!"

"The way I see it -"

"Be quiet Ricky."

Ricky drew breath

"I'll need your piece of land."

"But - "

"A crop on our hands we can't sell! Interest on loans to pay! Borrowings. Debts to service -"

"It's *always worked before*." Ricky interrupted.

"What do you think the security for the hospital and the planes was! Land! The workers' wages? How will I pay them?"

"The bank -"

"!You think we're surrounded by well-wishers?"

"Why don't they have to take the crop?"

"Because *we* contracted to supply it. They didn't contract to take it! Read the small print boy."

Ricky nodded. "And they won't take what they can't pass on. That's why they've given us time to change without invoking the penalty clause," he said quietly.

"You're beginning to get it. We are no different from common settlers with Management Agreements over our heads."

"We *can't* be!"

"What do you think we have if not a Management Agreement?" Victor shouted. "We are no more secure than the lowland rice farmers who took BANCOM's Improvement Loans to buy compulsory fertilizer to grow high yield *Masagana 99!* Look at them now! Debt ridden tenants on their own land! Like us!" He covered his eyes with his hand. "Profit is nothing to do with land ownership: it's land management! I don't want anyone to lose their job because of this."

Ricky hovered by the door.

"How can I help?"

"Order some flowers for your mother – from the Americans. Get out"

Think. Need time. Must think.

"Did Mr. Garvay and Mr. Colman really have to go?" Efigenia asked. "I managed to get in lobster! Were they good to you?"

"They offered us a good deal on polythene shrouds," Victor nodded.

There was a ring at the bell.

"Flowers for Mrs. Salcedo."

She read the card.

"Oh how charming!"

"We'll have the lobster ourselves Efigenia." Victor assured her, walking to the door.

"Are you going out?"

"I need to think - "

Soon Victor found himself back at the packing sheds where the day had started. He parked in its shadow. A young woman clutching a bottle of Fanta walked past him. Her daily treat. When she had a day off she'd probably listen to records with a girlfriend on a treasured record player, perhaps jointly owned. He watched her vanish in the trees. If she were not on the plantation she would have been a *bed spacer* in town, one of the myriad workers paying for the right to unfurl a straw mat on a space on a floor when the previous occupant arose for a night shift. Now she would be saving for her own gas burner and cooking utensils. If she stayed, if S.D.C.I. did not fold, she might one day be on 650 a month. He got out of his pickup, walked a little.

5.45. Sunset. He could hear a guitar from a hut. Curfew on the plantation was not till 9pm but people went to bed early, most eating their evening meal at 5pm. They were asleep by the time the discos in town would be starting up.

Returning to his pickup Victor switched on the lights. The guitar had ceased. A lone beam from a flashlight glanced through the trees. He backed away from the packing shed, the features of his plantation appearing and disappearing in his heads as the vehicle bumped from rut to rut. He drove half a mile then, in the grip of compulsion got out and walked into the banana thicket. The dead trunks, basis of his free fertilizer, were slippery, rotten underfoot and the 'arms' of bananas hanging waiting on the cableway menaced him. *What* was important? He returned to the pickup, the engines' familiar roar a comfort. "Dear God," he prayed. "*Spare my plantation.*" He flexed his fingers. "I know I have turned my back on you – I don't deny – but my family – these workers. Don't punish them because of me." He switched off the engine and tried to remember a potent prayer of Efigenia's but it wouldn't come. "*Help me,*" he reasoned with God. "Help *them*!" He punched the steering wheel. "Let the hospital go – if you can get me off the loan – *but keep the plantation.*" No point in being coy. "Ok I knew about the atrocities and I promise there will be no more and I'm sorry." He nodded. "I can't give the land back. How can I? I don't know where the people went. The point *is,*" he said desperately staring up at the dark sky, "I really will try. If you will only spare my plantation!"

Before getting into bed that night he knelt down and tried again.

"It's nice to see you praying," Efigenia smiled.

"Ssshh!" He prayed, waiting for a suggestion. Finally it came. He got up.

"I may have to go to Manila for a few days," he said calmly, getting into bed. "Will you have a Mass said? For the family's intentions?"

Chapter Seven

Eight lanes of traffic roared below the pedestrian bridge where Victor stood squinting at a banner "Manila – City of Man" which flapped in dense fumes opposite another: "The Philippines – a Nation Re-born". His eyes smarted, his throat felt tight. Below him a bus jammed with sweating Filipinos lurched backfiring across eight lanes of the wide boulevard of unzoned traffic, cement trucks, half covered jeepneys, their passengers' heads forced out into the fumes. He turned, coughing on the spot. In one direction, the financial towers of Makati rose from the smog. In another, the tips of the walled city Intramuros could be made out sinking. He began walking. "HONESTY IS THE BEST POLICY" said a hoarding. Beside it an elderly man was berating a newsvendor for the benefit of a tourist: "The price is written here," he told the tourist. "One peso. We are honest people. But at the same time you should be vigilant." Victor passed him. A beggar woman pushed her legs out in a manner to inconvenience bridge users. He stepped over her. "Despite the efforts of the President and the First Lady there are still elements of the Old Society here!" the elderly man's voice followed him. The stink of the traffic surging below, its relentless noisy barrage, oppressed him as did the presence of people around him, fighting to get on busses which took off leaning unevenly, children running parallel, offering newspapers to the drivers.

A blue air conditioned "LOVE BUS" bus was blocking the intersection, coloured hearts dotted around the phrase Metro Manila Transport Corp as if riding it were a marvellous adventure. He hated Manila. The bus began to move, further hearts at the back urging "USE BUS" and

"SAVE GAS". People hemmed him in: youths in freshly pressed bellbottoms, clutching cheap satchels, heading for backstreet "Colleges"; men in tight T-shirts gripping newspaper cuttings, looking for Agencies that would take them on to crew ships, do construction work in Oman… They surged jauntily past him, undeterred by the 80% charge the Agencies would levy. Only the chance to *get out* mattered.

He took a taxi, wanting to be gone as soon as possible but three things had to be done in Manila. He had already made one phone call. He was expected.

"Makati." He gave the address.

Different areas of the city fell away: finally they arrived and the taxi stopped.

"Here you are, Sir."

The entire block was banks.

"Which is the one I asked you for?"

"Go inside Sir. Ask."

Last time he had been in Makati, he had been on the up.

He skated across the lobby floor. Rather than answer his question, the receptionist waved a painted hand at the gold nameplates by the lift: PDCPW, Far East Bank and Trust Company, PCI …. He entered the lift. He must go into this meeting with a positive attitude. The loan needed re-negotiating on the basis that he had decided to sell the planes. This must be done without mentioning his problems. He caught sight of himself in the mirror.

Stepping out of the lift he checked his watch. Below him, like toys, cars sat in lines, a solitary cab moving along a deserted street in and out of sun and shadow between the blocks of power and wealth. If this went well, perhaps ask for a further loan? Think positive. He knocked at the suite.

"Come - " He pushed the door. The manager rose, extended his hand. "Victor! This is very sad!"

Had he guessed something? The ground plan of S.D.C.I. Holdings was spread on his desk! Battening his nerves, Victor crossed briskly to him, shook hands: "I see you haven't got neighbours yet," he said jovially, indicating far below a vacant lot high with tropical grass.

"Yes very sad," repeated the manager, sitting. "However what can I do for you?"

Find a position of strength before mentioning the planes!

"I need a buyer for my current crop of large Cavendish."

"I take it you get the papers in Mindanao?" the manager asked lifting down his bound collection of Herald Tribunes. "You will have difficulty finding anyone to take them at this time." He smacked a headline. "See here. Iran Halts Import of Luxury Goods. See? They've had some sort of religious revolution and are kicking everyone out – except the Japanese who are hanging onto their petrochemical plant by the skin of their teeth." Victor waited. "Right now transnational companies are looking for ways to lighten their commitments," the manager continued. "To be frank, you should hang onto those planes for when spraying comes back."

Victor controlled his face and feelings.

"I rather imagine you came up here needing to sell not just your crop but the planes." The manager tapped S.D.C.I.'s file. "And don't look so mystified. No one's peached. All I needed to guess was that your buyer'd quit taking the crop off you. For how long by the way? A year?"

"I'm sure a less particular transnational company - " Victor began. "Say the English, say *Castle & Cooke* or *Reynolds* -"

"*Reynolds* are American."

"Wouldn't carp about pesticide levels."

"This is nothing to do with pesticides," the manager said firmly. "But I might add, your secondhand planes have enough interest outstanding to meet the cost of a new plane."

Somehow Victor could not grasp what the man was saying.

"There are two issues here," the manager stated. "But the only thing I am concerned with though I would have been pleased to help you with the other matters as a friend – is your repayment to the bank of the loan on your planes." His hand passed over the section of land which had been the security for the loan, the *flattest*, the best part … If he thought he was going to get his hands on *that* he'd rip up every last banana plant first! But he couldn't because the agreement had stated the land "as is", meaning it would revert fully planted and equipped with cableway to the mortgagor.

"Sorry, what did you say?"

"That when *Del Mundo* find new markets to replace Iran you will need those planes. So I suggest you find the money and continue paying."

Victor said nothing.

"Because if you renege, we sell your land to the highest bidder."

"Which could be me."

"At an enhanced rate? I doubt it. Now that the land has title. Don't look so crestfallen. Reverses are to be expected in business. How is your wife?" Victor shook his head. "Come! This is a temporary set-back. The price of bananas might rise -" Victor nodded. "You must make representations to the Americans. Have you done?"

"No."

"Contacts at their Embassy? Who leans on *United Brands* -"

"It's *Del Mundo*. Not *United Brands* -"

"Did you compromise Coleman and Garvay?"

"I showed them my horse."

"Should have taken them to a brothel!"

Victor felt the man disparage him as one who had lost his cutting edge.

"Try to get your hands on some money Victor," the manager rose, "You have such a fine family."

Unable to smile Victor moved to the door: "You may think I'm shot to pieces -"

"You do seem to be slipping. Tell you what -" the manager softened. "See you in the lobby of the Manila Hotel tomorrow night. Tell me how you get on!"

As Victor left the room the manager picked up the phone.

Outside the sun beat down on his neck. Two women, umbrellas protecting them, crossed the shimmering road. The manager was wrong about pesticides. In a *Banana Growers Weekly,* left in the lounge of the *Valemon* where he was staying, he'd seen prototypes of the polythene sheets widely in use elsewhere. He looked up and down the empty street for a cab. Nothing moved but a *peon* in worn dungarees slowly sweeping a twig broom into a broken shovel. Climbing the kerb onto a glinting pavement Victor followed the women hoping they were heading for a bus stop. Probably workers who travelled to and from Makati by air-conditioned Express Love Bus.

Makati – a word which sounded evil - like Brazilian voodoo…

The women ahead walked slower and slower then stood, feet shifting on the hot pavement by a sign on a concrete post. *Pasay, Ermita, Quiapo, Santa Cruz…* Waiting in the heat, Victor figured. Garvey and Coleman's talk about "home concern" about pesticides had been rubbish. He didn't supply the US. They used Central and South America. There'd been no mention of the Japanese kicking up. That meant some other grower, harder to bump than he, had taken his spot supplying the Japanese market: someone whose fruit had previously gone to Iran. Sweat ran down his neck. Like the tropical canopy in vacant lots, everything was cloying, climbing on its neighbour towards the light.

That morning, before going to the bank, in the quiet of San Agustin church, the tree of his pride had come crashing to the forest floor. As light streamed in and sun-loving plants had sprung, he'd yearned forgiveness, a fresh start. But seeds from the giant *Tapang* had rooted: their creepers breaking cover everywhere. He'd known *for sure* about the 'atrocities'. *He'd* asked men to 'clear the land'. He *knew* the CHDF contained 'elements'. In the church he'd heard a sound, had looked up and seen a sparrow had flitted in. *If he repented properly, surely God would help him through the meeting?* The sparrow had perched, chirping loudly, on the rusty chain that let down the chandelier. Surely a sign, an omen? He looked at the ceiling above, like those in the Italian churches his wife had dragged him into. *If he went to confession now,* it would put the seal on his new resolution. He licked his lips. The thought of the priest's hand descending, the words: "I absolve you. Go in peace" tempting. He could feel the centuries of prayer that had soaked into the stone floor around him.

When the bus came, he climbed onto it. So much for prayer! Good job he hadn't bothered with confession!

The bus waited at lights hanging in a deserted intersection. He wiped his forehead. He needed to set up meetings, find buyers for the crop. But would word have gone ahead? Would people be "out", though secretaries would be polite about it? The only way to do business in Manila was to have a person of power introduce you and that should have been his bank manager... *Anyone* he met would ask him if he had spoken to his bank manager, and if he said Yes, the fact he was now alone, asking them personally, would make him doubly untouchable.

He alighted in Manila. On all sides people were eating. Leaning against lampposts; under tarps stretched between buildings, sitting on the walls of flower beds, snacking on scraps wrapped in palm leaves... Laughing. Talking. He pushed between office workers, sat at an empty metal table in a crowded alley, a small gutter running by its wall. At once the owner reached a bowl off a table passed it through a bucket, shook off the water, dipped it in his tureen, flicked two dumplings in and banged it down in front of Victor, his rag swiping at the puddle running towards him. With two fingers the man snatched a spoon from a jar and wiped it on his singlet. Around Victor office girls lifted spoonfuls to their mouths, extracted gristle from their teeth with extreme delicacy, their conversation buoyant. He moved his foot. A cockroach darted off and squeezed itself in a crack by the wall. In bright sun on the sidewalk a tourist family were arguing, the man's shirt open on a glistening pink dome. No one looked at him. Humanity surged endlessly by. It would be too late to see anyone now. Offices would be closed 'til four in the afternoon and who would see him then? But he must try and make arrangements for tomorrow.

In the dark of the confessional, Jack concentrated.

"When did this happen?"

"Last week Father."

"You say – 'Things being the way they are – a death occurred'."

"Yes Father."

"Are you saying you killed someone?"

The man hesitated. Jack sensed him resisting his questioning.

"Did someone ask you to do what you did?"

"Partly."

"And you had to do it for the sake of your occupation?"

"Perhaps."

Jack paused. It was up to the man, soldier, hired assassin or executioner, how honest he wanted to be with God.

"Were you told to – do what you did – or was there a moment of choice?"

The man hesitated.

"Could you have – carried out your work without – that kind of thing happening on that occasion?"

"I think so Father."

"I see. And now you are sorry?"

"Yes father."

"Make an *Act of Contrition* and for your penance think about *what it was you wanted* that made you do the thing you did. Think what it was that made you turn from God. And which you want most. That thing or what you have come here to get. Your peace of mind and reconciliation with God."

He felt the man's dissatisfaction with what he had said: as if it had been inadequate, insensitive, misplaced.

"When we sin, we turn from God and choose to live without him," Jack said simply. "We can sin all we like but it won't make us happy."

"It stops our stomach," the man whispered. "My heart belongs to God but my stomach to my employer."

There was a shaft of light as the confessional door opened and closed behind the man.

Jack waited in the confessional. People came to confession in the Cathedral rather than their own parish church because they were not known. One hour to go. Though he could not see the penitent and fought against putting faces to voices, he was beginning to recognise some. That men killed with such ease suggested a situation where obliterating each other was a normal facet of existence, far removed from the occasional murder in England which brought teams of men out combing hills, late night newscasts and photofits. The English lied, fornicated, misled in the pursuit of *happiness*. But the things these killers wanted were the things ordinary people had. They were in the power of others who used them for their ends. This much was clear. Victor's advice that he avoid "going off half-cocked" had restrained him so far as had Efigenia's well meant: "Avoid complex issues".

At best, in one sermon he had attempted to plead the cause of integrity saying: "*Sin* is not a commodity like - butter or brick. The word means 'sin' comes from the Latin, *'sine'*, meaning "without". The word "sincere" comes from *'sin cere' - meaning* - without wax," he had explained to a flat faced congregation. "Because in Roman times when marble statutes had been damaged, crafty salesmen would push candle wax in the cracks to make them look whole. When work was said to be sincere, it meant – of a piece –genuine – or whole. Or as we say, holy." He checked his watch.

How did they articulate the concepts "Thou Shalt Not Kill" with "You see Father, things being the way they are…"? They had an affection for their Faith: not an intellectual but an emotional response to it, absorbed along with mothers' milk before the formation of words, in the silence waiting while mothers finished urgent prayers. Their belief in God's loyalty to them was the gift of those women who took refuge in prayer from the hardness of men. For a man to deny God would be to return home and murder his mother.

But the more he got to grips with their attitude, the more uncomfortable he felt boxing them into corners with traditional objectives, with logical arguments the penitent could not win. How fair were they?

"I regret the man's life is over, yes Father. And that my life is not pleasing to God -"

"Are you saying it is *inconvenient* to you that killing is a sin?"

"It was necessary to kill him."

"Then why confess it?"

The man waited, then:

"Because I want absolution."

"How long is it since your last confession?"

"Three weeks."

"Had similar events occurred then?"

"Yes."

"But you were sorry -"

117

"Last time I decided I wouldn't do it again."

"And what do you think now?"

"I have been thinking Father and it seems -" the man paused. Was he now going to be penalised for the honesty of his own thought? "It seems Father very likely that – that – "

"Unless you can tell me that you do not intend to cause unnecessary death, although I would like to give absolution, I must withhold it."

The man had risen.

Had he been wrong to force him to *think?*

Suddenly the door to the confessional slid open and a woman knelt before him: "Father – I want you to help me find my grandchildren -" This was not the way confessions usually began.

"Come to the house and see me afterwards."

"The church people on the beach told me not to speak of it openly –"

"Very well." Jack listened. As the woman unfurled her story, things began falling into place. Surely this was the woman in the bloodstained dress who'd turned up at the Salcedo's the day he'd arrived: the other side of the 'my stomach belongs to my employer' coin. Her voice was rising.

"Please lower your voice."

"Four children! Violeta has baby Cresmalin. Please God Edgar is with Adan …."

"But *how* can the Church help?" Jack whispered.

"You have maps."

This was true. The only accurate maps of upriver villages, remote settlements in wildernesses in parts of South America and Africa had been drawn by missionaries. Indeed governments constantly pestered them for information.

"You must help me look for them!"

"What have you done so far?"

"I have prayed to the Blessed Virgin Mary at the Shrine. Every day."

"What *physical* steps have you taken?"

"I walk."

"What part did you come from?" Jack asked in a low voice, scrabbling for a pencil. "When we finish, go outside and pray with your head down as if saying your penance. Do you understand?"

"Yes Father. From my place I came down a road with the sun behind me in the morning."

"What kind of road? Were there busses on it? Trucks? Was there something on the trucks? Pineapples? Timber?"

"I don't know. When I heard traffic coming, I stepped off the road."

Jack checked his watch.

"Was it a straight road or did it bend?"

"Perhaps."

"So the sun was behind you?" He scribbled.

"At first. Then over my left shoulder. But it passed overhead so I seemed to be walking towards it on my right."

"How long were you walking?"

"Long."

"How did you get to the road from where you had been living?"

"I cut through the bush on small tracks."

"How long did you walk?"

That evening taking a map and compass, he marked out two likely roads and began circling areas of 'unclaimed land' from which the woman might have come if the sun had been behind her at the outset and she'd travelled approximately south southwest. "These are the sections -" he marked them, "to look for tracks leading off…"

This second day in Manila had shown Victor there was no hope. Behind him, the city was lit up; before him, Manila Bay spread in a polluted furnace. Out on the water, ships kept their distance. Behind them the sun was going down.

He walked a little, followed by a youth who'd been leaning on a coconut tree, watching him. The youth asked for a cigarette, his eyes following Victor's hands to his pocket. He would almost have welcomed being robbed for the human contact!

In a flurry of horns Victor stepped into the road, taxis screeching to avoid him. He waved them on, thinking of the quietness of *his* beach, the silence of *his* plantation. Maybe the bank manager had forgotten him, his parting invitation a throw-away remark. But what had he to lose? They might not let even him into the Hotel, sweaty and red from walking. No one arrived at the Manila Hotel on foot: they came in air-conditioned cabs, usually straight from the airport or from another hotel. Anyway it was all too late. Who cared? Certainly not God! He'd prayed hard that day and what good had it done him? Ahead For Hire cars streamed under a banner welcoming visitors to the *Philippine International Convention Centre*: bringing money to feed those grave-markers of imported wealth, Makati's skyscrapers. Finally reaching the hotel he stepped straight past the door boys, smart in white uniforms but probably living in Tondo or some other slum and lacking the confidence to challenge a man on foot with a soiled shirt.

Inside the lobby was cold, its marble floor broken by carefully placed palms. Victor crossed to a red sofa, plumped himself down, stretching his legs out to display pointed dusty shoes. Around him, small clutches of sofas had been arranged to encourage groups to form, the carpet's deep pile hushing sounds. Tourists moved in ones and twos to enquire at the guest reception whether the taxi had charged the right price or to boast about the dollar rate they'd gotten or drop their keys in the slot. A bell hop stared at Victor's outstretched legs. Four thin Filipinos with violin cases hurried past. He was half an hour early.

Outside, door boys hurried forward as a two-tone Lincoln Continental eased itself close to the marble steps. They flung the doors open, saluting as a man climbed out, sailed past them and stood looking around the lobby. He nodded towards a man setting up a music stand. The man shook his head, indicting a bell boy. With his eyes, the bell boy indicated the crown of Victor's head appearing over the crest of the sofa.

"Bless my soul!" the man said loudly, approaching, extending his hand. "Victor Salcedo!"
Aware he did not know the man, Victor got to his feet.
"Don't say you don't remember me!"
"I – um -"
"Margolas. You're the dark horse Victor!"

He snapped his fingers. Quickly a sofa was pushed forward.

"Are you here for the meeting?"

"I have an appointment with -"

"Best thing to happen to Mindanao this century! Two *Budweisers* boy - Where are you staying?"

"The *Valemon*."

Margolas grinned. "Playing your cards close to your chest I see. Staying out of the mainstream. But let me get you a room here. There's someone I'd like you to meet -"

He crossed to Reception, had a brief conversation.

"No good," he said returning. "It'll have to be the Hilton. I've booked you in."

"I don't want any misunderstandings," Victor stated. "I'm here because my bank manager turned me down for –"

"No vision bank managers," Margolas frowned. "What was your project?"

"Agri-business." Victor downed his beer. "The Cavendish isn't a native variety. It's prone to pests."

"Oh! My apologies! I thought you were here for the meeting but – Hoh! Here they are! -" He quickly rose. "And we're not talking fruit!" Four Americans in dark suits, obviously straight from the airport, were passing through the lobby. "If you're interested I might manage to swing something your way -" He bent to Victor: "Get round to the Hilton. I'll show up later." He moved quickly away.

From another sofa, the bank manager watched Victor lean forward, help himself to Margolas' unfinished beer. He waited a few minutes. When the Americans and Margolas had gone, he crossed to Victor.

"Sorry I'm late. How did things go?" He sat down. Any joy with *Proctor and Gamble?*"

"No," Victor said flatly. "Did you find anything for me?"

"I'm still looking but - "

"I see -" Victor rose.

"Are you still at the *Valemon?* In case -"

"I'm moving to the Hilton." He lingered, trying to read the manager's face.

"Right on United Nations Avenue," the man said drily. "All the important places." He indicated the empty bottles. "Who've you been drinking with?"

"His name slips me." Victor said, looking towards the door. "I'm off now."

The manager remained staring after Victor. Margolas couldn't have been honest with him when he stated his interest in Victor was slight. The Americans with the airport limo were clearly of consequence. And Victor had been cocky. Yet on the other hand there were vacancies in this hotel ....so Margolas wasn't spending much on him.

In the Hilton, Victor struggled with changing moods. Was it possible he knew Margolas? From when the plantation had been set up? Sighing he breathed in the musty smell of water that had dripped from an air conditioner onto a heavy shag carpet, and stale smoke allowed to collect in the curtains. Had Margolas mistaken him for someone else and did it matter? He fiddled with the air conditioner 'til it came on with a loud judder, sending cold air into the room. The point was, the man had something to offer.

Convincing himself things were looking up, he showered, had a meal and charged it, the sense of relief palpable; the feeling, as he crossed Rizal Park in the cooler air and walked up General Luna, almost bright. Finding himself at Manila Cathedral and fearing he had misjudged God, he entered, said a few prayers to be on the safe side, then returned to his room to wait.

At 11.00 pm sharp, his room phone rang.

"Gentleman to see you in reception."

"Send him up."

Victor glanced round the room, which despite his efforts, still looked like a bedroom.

Margolas entered. He looked flushed. Important.

"Have you somewhere I can -?"

Victor pushed the two bedside cabinets together. Margolas spread out a large map which Victor instantly recognised as Mindanao. "Sit. Sit Victor." He patted the bed, his manner suggesting there was work to be done. "Take a good look at the map."

Victor looked. His holdings, S.D.C.I., were clearly marked. So the man *did* know who he was. But so were B.F. Goodrich, Union Carbide, Goodyear Tire and Rubber's. Everyone's was there: Dolephil, followed by (Castle & Cooke) in brackets. Even the percentages of holdings of 3rd party interests were in the margins.

"You're very thorough."

"I mean to be." Margolas looked up then down again. "Here you see – with SMC, Nestle Corporation of Switzerland are putting up a 350 million peso coffee processing plant at the Phivedec industrial estate in Villanueva, site of the Kawasaki sintering plant. Not bad, eh?"

"No."

"51% owned by Nestle and exporting to Asian markets and China."

"Yes."

Fascinated but frightened, Victor waited. Why tell him?

"Now let me show you another map."

Victor's heart jumped. It pertained only to North Davao Province and reached as far as the borders of Agusan del Sur and Bukidnon and North Cotobato. "Apart from encroachment by Stanfilco (alias Castle & Cooke) you alone have power here." Victor nodded. Too close. Too close! Margolas looked him straight in the eye. "You saved us a trip by being here." Victor swallowed. Margolas pointed at a space between blocks of titled ownership.

"I think you know what this is."

"The homeland of 50,000 *Ata-Manobo* tribesmen!" Victor replied firmly.

"Not what I had in mind." Margolas smiled, his finger moving up a forested mountain slope, stroking the paper as if it were an incline.

"This, keep it under your hat, is one of the largest copper ore deposits in Asia. It is estimated we could take out 25,000 tons of ore a day for the next hundred years."

Victor flexed his feet.

"I don't expect you to take my word for it -" Margolas pulled Articles of Incorporation from his briefcase, straightened them for Victor to read. He glanced. Were they planning a 250 hectare open-pit copper mine just north of him, *on his doorstep?*

"It will be the North Davao Copper Ore Extraction Corp. NDCOEC."

"I've heard nothing of this."

"Why would you? We've already put in a road."

His finger stabbed at the region Victor imagined the woman in the black dress had fled.

"Why tell me?"

"Your name came up." He edged closer to Victor. "The Government is *very* keen on this project."

Victor looked woodenly at the floor.

"Come. Get up! I have someone for you to meet!"

Sick to his stomach Victor climbed into a taxi after Margolas. He was being taken to meet someone who would confuse him with detail, make an offer he couldn't understand, force him to sign papers in the middle of the night and .... *They wanted his plantation.* Beyond the window the Manila Yacht Club, the Cultural Centre of the Philippines, the Design Centre all slid by, their immense concrete scale dwarfing him, making him feel insignificant. His place, *his house even* would be levelled! JCBs would come; it would be a machine dump. Or would they use his house as an office? His eyes danced in desperation from the cab, to be mocked by The Trade and Exhibition Centre glowering in its magnificence, the grandeur of the PICC Delegation Building, the Plenary Hall .... floodlit fountains shouting: 'Money! Power!' But what was Margolas saying?

" - - a decision maker *yourself,* a man with local influence."

"Oh -?"

"Your *opinion,* your *input* here, would be valuable."

Maybe they didn't want his plantation!? He stepped from the cab.

"Because we intend to get that copper ore out!"

Entering the Century Park Sheraton, Margolas led him to the bar: "I give you Victor Salcedo!"

"*Victor Salcedo*!" A man turned. "We've heard good reports about you!"

"Don't embarrass him," Margolas joked. "At first he didn't recognise me!"

"Didn't recognise the director of PANAMIN?"
Bile rose in Victor's throat. The Presidential Assistant on National Minorities. PANAMIN.

"Let's sit." An orchestra was striking up. "Antonio Marabut," the man extended his hand.
"Also Presidential Minorities Commission. What'll you have?" At the next table three American ladies in flip-flops, were drinking from carved-out pineapples, staring at the banner: JOHNNY TIROLLAS & the EMPERADORES. Victor ordered a scotch.

"Basically," Marabut began, drawing a map on a napkin. "This is your land – and this here the land needed for the mine. Free land."

"It's spotted with Visayan settlers," Victor stated. "Apart from the tribals. Who own it."

"Where a man of your knowledge, your *experience* can use *tact,*" Marabut continued. "We understand you have excellent relationships with the *Ata*: something not easily arrived at."

"I buy a certain amount of *ipil-ipil* from them."

"We hear they have to give you a quota of 40,000 *ipil-ipil* saplings *a year* for the privilege of staying on the land."

"For the privilege of my protection."

"Whatever it takes."

"Whereas," Victor said loudly. "*Ata* not under my protection pay PANAMIN 50% of their harvest, plus other fees, *and* provide free labour on projects, in order to –"

The women at the next table turned to stare.

"Yes. In our own ways you and I have both brought peace to the area," Marabut agreed, smiling at the ladies. "You know the *Ata* well. You are respected by them – which is why we thought you might like to – and this is purely your option – look after their interests in this matter – *along with us.* Of course we can manage without you. But the mine will cause disruption and we are anxious to minimise it. Yet at the same time, *the mine will go through.*"

"In some parts of the country," Margolas said gently. "Terrible things happen to tribals where there is development. Army ravages -"

Victor remained silent.

"The Presidential Assistant for National Minorities has of course sole responsibility for bringing about a situation where the army does not *have* to be called in." He smiled at Victor. "And these people have no title. Do we understand each other?"

Victor closed his eyes.

"We thought you might like to – take part in *facilitating* this National work," Margolas suggested. "In a humane way. Funds will be made available to you." He named the exact sum outstanding on the two planes. "Immediately."

"I'm not killing anyone."

"We hope not!"

Two hours later the ladies had gone, the bar area was closed off and the tone of the meeting had changed.

"You will not kill any tribal because they will move this way," Margolas stated, sweeping his hand across the napkin from the direction of the mine site to the Paquibato area.

"Why will they move?"

"Because they will be fleeing."

"The fighting," Marabut explained. "Amongst themselves. Which you will instigate."

Victor looked down.

"We can offer you help with your current banana crop too – Another drink? In fact we'll take it off your hands. Now."

"There is a colossal amount of international finance here," Margolas pressed on. "The big boys are falling over themselves to get in but again, not meaning to criticize the American Missionary Fathers *on your patch* …."

"The point *is*," Marabut interrupted. "Before the consortium of banks releases the finance, a United Nations Commission will be visiting the area to make sure it's clear."

"I see."

"Any hint of atrocities and the deal will cry off. So we are looking to totally clear this entire area," his hand swept across the tribal lands, the mine site and Paquibato. "Before the UN Commission visits." Marabut and Margolas eyed Victor. "That's the offer."

Victor shook his head.

"Then we'll try your neighbour. Apparently Stanfilco's stood him up on this year's harvest too -"

"I can't do it."

"Fine. That's fine Victor. My mistake." Marabut pulled his case out from under the table and stood up. "What do you think the world's made of? Sugar paste?" he said angrily. "We're going to have this mine. If you clear the land, chances are it'll be done in a humane fashion. Regardless, this time next year, it'll be operational. The

UN Commission are coming 1st November. All Saints Day. *Operation All Saints."*

"Let me think about it."

"Hardly."

Margolas stood. "It's dying in here. Let's go to the club."

As 4.00 a.m. came around Victor was fairly drunk. A slender girl in sequinned dress was sitting on the arm of his chair, eyes fixed on him. He turned to her.

"I am a married man."

"Yes Sir."

She remained sitting.

Through the haze he saw a group of western journalists propping each other by the bar and beyond them *his bank manager* in conversation with Margolas and Marabut. Suddenly the manager walked over.

"So your debt on the planes is taken care of. Congratulations."

Victor yawned. The band started to play.

"Thought for a second you'd lost your touch."

"Back on course, eh?" he said blearily.

"You're on 'hold' Victor 'til All Saints Day – when your debt will be discharged."

"I haven't agreed yet," he said loudly.

Marabut came and sat next to him. "Cigar?"

Victor shook his head.

"We can make all kinds of support available to you. In the interests of *national security."*

"Of *course."*

"When trouble develops PANAMIN will establish a special *Ata* settlement project some way west; the military will stand by you and issue both warring sides with automatic weapons *in their own defence -"*

Are they actually asking *me,* Victor shook his head, to start a war?

"The 59th PC battalion's commander will take orders from you, given your overall understanding of the situation and y*our concern for the Ata.* Naturally it is in the army's interest to keep peace in the area -"

Victor blew his nose.

"Strife will not be tolerated."

"No."

"If you need to open up a third front, you have the INP force – 100% Visayan and already at loggerheads with the *Atas* -" Marabut pulled out the Terms and Conditions of Agreement again. Victor could barely focus. "See here?" he smacked the paper. "Antonio Marabut and Jaime Margolas – sole Filipino directors of the mining venture. Given the sensitive siting of the mine, it was obvious to the government which agencies should handle it."

"You'll buy this year's banana crop off me at a cash price? And pay off my loans?"

"If you're with us. And deliver. Or shall we go to your neighbour?"

"My neighbour?"

"Of your plantation. If it survives."

In a moment of clarity before falling asleep Victor dreamt he heard the voices of Garvay and Coleman and Marabut and Margolas and his bank manager coming from bushes in his garden, all muttering about the mine, making up stories about pesticides to trick him! He reached for an aspirin. But the iron ore *did* exist because, before he'd been too far gone, he'd heard the western journalists at the bar talking openly of Central Mindanao copper ore.

And that was before Margolas had bought them a drink and reminded them there were release dates on bits of information and if they jumped the gun they'd find their cables censored and their work permits withdrawn. He crunched the aspirin. It was a special Club where the foreign press were allowed in to be fed strategic morsels of information ....

"You have to be *very careful* in this bar," Margolas had warned him, pointing at them. "Word has to get out to bring foreign capital in. But when *we're* ready." He nodded at them. "It's every Filipino's duty to – help open up the land." He placed his hand on Victor's shoulder. "I'm sure you'll agree. And we've turned to you because we need a man who can *shift rocks with kid gloves.* You could end up in Manila."

Victor got up to switch off the air conditioner. It was wrong, the thing they were asking. He gazed from the window. 4 hours to make up his mind. To take the opportunity or leave it. Below, Manila slept in yellow white concrete, sun glinting off the daggers of Makati. For a long time he stood looking out. In an hour the city would come to life.

Chapter Eight

After a breakfast of scrambled eggs, bacon strips and French toast, things looked different. Victor leaned back in his chair, the hotel's buffet gleaming in the morning sun, light dancing off crystal glasses, chafing dishes, brass samovars... He would do it! He rose to refill his coffee. A tourist mooching amongst the yoghurts smiled at him. He nodded back, helped himself to the morning paper and sat, stirring his coffee and tapping the saucer three times with his spoon for luck. Why not? He couldn't sell the horse: no racing history and too old. If word even got out that he was *trying* to sell the horse his neighbours'd know he was up against the ropes and move in on him.

Straight after breakfast, he made the phone call.

"I'm with you."

Margolas hesitated for a beat. "Good decision," he said slowly.

"I'll be going back home this morning."

"Get straight onto it."

"You won't be disappointed."

"I hope not. For your sake."

On the flight home, surrounded by ordinary people, the very sort he was being asked to displace, his mood plunged. A knitting woman pulled her arm off the rest to give him more room, smiled at him revealing teeth that needed work. But no killing. He had always said it. But he was being asked to unleash violence on an unprecedented scale on his own doorstep! It would ruin him in the eyes of his family and would Marabout and Margolas, alias PANAMIN, protect him after he'd outgrown his usefulness? Or would they take his plantation on top of it? But if he *didn't?* He became aware of the stewardess asking him if he were alright? She was an ordinary girl, probably from a family like his own but poorer, leaning over him, her breath stale as if she were hungry. He shut his eyes. Then someone *else* would do it. Someone *else* would clear the land more violently than he and he'd be stuck with the planes, the debt, the crop; his family would become homeless...! At a tap on the arm he opened his eyes. The stewardess and knitting woman were looking at him with concern, the stewardess offering him a glass of water and the woman producing a lone mint from her knitting bag.

They had offered him a lifeline. He took the mint. Why? If they'd put in a road, if that were even *true,* why had they stopped? Only one family, to his knowledge, had been displaced. Had they run into difficulty? A man who could *"shift rocks with kid gloves."* That's what they'd said about him. If they could have done it themselves, they wouldn't have asked him. That meant they couldn't do it "appropriately" - meaning without publicity, international scandal, the project crying off and the funds going elsewhere. Looked at like that, the Philippine Government, the President and Powerful Interests were dependent on him.

He accepted a brandy from the stewardess.

Yet along with his bank manager, they had him over a barrel. Yes. But they wouldn't have bothered if they didn't regard him as competent. He took another swallow. A man who, in other circumstances, would have been on a par with them!

Taking a large swallow of the brandy, he sensed a curtain sliding back to reveal a more virile version of himself, which had been held in check by moral and social strictures he had never been consulted about, strictures imposed from without which had shackled initiative. Wasn't what they were asking no different from what he'd already done but demanding greater cunning?

The plane touched down and taxied. He reached the knitting woman's bag down from the overhead locker. It was a cheap plastic carrier containing foodstuffs probably, gifts from a relative she had taken pineapples to.

He stepped into the Terminal. Such a woman, her very pineapples: how could he plan to upend her? *But if it were not him it would be someone else.*

Across the terminal he saw Efigenia leaning anxiously on Ricky's arm, peering about.

"Victor! Victor!" She began to hurry across.

But what if he tried and failed? Had *they* given up because it couldn't be done? Was he just a last shot? With everything still to lose?

"This wasn't necessary!" he embraced Efigenia, aware of Ricky watching him closely. "You needn't have come to the airport."

"Ricky wouldn't say why you'd gone. I was worried."

"It was nothing." He settled in the car. "There was an issue with oversupply. I had to sell elsewhere."

"And did you?"

"Of course. A government department took this year's crop off me for use as emergency supplies."

"But that's *wonderful!*" Efigenia grasped his hand. "You see Ricky? Your father's charisma! What was the emergency? A hurricane disaster?"

"Some place where crops had been destroyed by rampaging tribesmen."

"So we carry on as before?"

"Absolutely."

"You are *wonderful*!"

Back home, Ricky followed him into his study. "O.K. So what about the planes?"

"Loan rolled over."

"*Why*?"

"The big bank manager, not *our* little twerp, had it that Garvey and Coleman gave us the sharp end. It was the Americans, not the Japanese who kicked up about pesticides. We just had a weak contract. So stronger growers' fruit went to *our* buyers in Japan while *we* got laid off. He told us we'd need the planes for when it blew over."

"So he rolled the debt?"

"There's more to it but you don't need to know -"

"I want to -"

"They've lost some markets in Iran. They need time to find more."

"Do we go along with the plastic sheaths?"

"We have to."

The exchange depressed Victor and thinking about it in his study rather than on the plane brought it home. They had to survive. It was alright for the poor. They could pick scraps off the street without losing face: precariousness made them grateful. But Efigenia would be terrified of poverty. Nor would any of them thank him for failure, come to that. But the *unfairness* of finding himself in this position; of having to deal with people who were rotten to the core, of being sucked into their evil ate him. It was PANAMIN's job, not his, to shift tribals to reserves and repossess or rather possess their land. They knew and he knew the *Atas* wouldn't go; there'd be a scandal; Church groups would get involved and the international press: then the project would fold and the country be denied the reserves it needed to get through the next hundred years. He was being forced by circumstance to accept an offer anyone in his position would have grabbed. It made you pity Judas, picked before he'd been formed in the womb.

Marabut stepped over the razor-sharp grass that had colonised the vacant lot and ran in a hollow carpet towards the road.

"What if he doesn't -"

"The man's desperate."

"But in *time*."

"Properly motivated – Victor will achieve."

Margolas pulled a tendril from his cuff. "Did you tell him the other thing?"

"Of course not. Just enough rope to swim ashore. He won't get back in though."

As night fell Victor became uneasy. *How was it to be done?* If he prayed, would God start the war to push the *Atas* westward? He'd helped him in Manila. Or did he have to take the branch he'd been offered? Maybe asking an *Ata* to kill an *Ata* was not as bad as setting Christian against Christian. They enjoyed fighting. Just don't ask them to commit adultery: that they punished with drowning! He picked up a pencil, flicked it in his fingers. Then laid the pencil down. Got up. They were right in Manila. He knew how to do it! 50,000? A mere football

137

crowd. And the *Ata* didn't believe in land ownership any more than the transnational companies. This would show them in Manila! Let no one doubt he was master of his universe!

He waited until everyone was asleep upstairs and the house quiet, then went to the cupboard where he kept his souvenirs of *Ata* weaponry, crouched, drew out a *surit-surit*, turned it in his hands. His thumb stroked its edge. It was of the sort exchanged between warring sides after the turmoil, usually burned at peace pacts… He took it to the light, put on his glasses.

The following day feeling more calm in his mind he went about his business in as normal a manner as possible, solicitous of minor details on the plantation, yet part of him wanted to sing. Surges of elation washed over him, marred only by the fact that he could not share his idea with anyone. Come evening, he slipped into an old jeep and went out 'for a breath'. Slowly he motored towards the hills. He would not kill anyone. He would throw something away. What others did, they did. Quietly the jeep entered the foothills and stopped. Victor wound down the window, listened. The tropical evening, giving way to night, hummed and clicked. Turning round, he picked up something from the back seat, quietly climbed from the jeep, pushing the door to. It clicked. He started to walk up the track. As it got higher, the light, even on the hill tops, was fading.

Below, in a clearing, he could make out roofs. He sat, waiting for dark. Vehicles now would have their lights on but his, if seen, lay where trucks often broke down. And people were not abroad at night. He listened. This was mixed *Ata* territory, some land having been taken by

Visayans for *usa kay baboy* or token payments. Far off a dog barked.

Approaching a hut, through the woven walls he saw a lamp had been lit and heard the sound of pots and a transistor radio. Visayans! No need to go further. But he waited. Already bats were flitting about, shapes growing dim. Steadying himself on one knee, he unwrapped the cloth, removed the *surit-surit* and aimed. *THWING!* The missile sped through the air and lodged in the split bamboo of the house. At once the pots stopped, the radio went dead, the lamp was blown out. He got to his feet, crept on.

At the first group of *Ata* dwellings, he tossed the *surit-surit* over the barricade. It landed between two houses.

Marabut passed the Mindanao Journal to Margolas: "Clever Victor!" He said. "It's a side item. Listen."

> "63 year old Visayan farmer, Segundino Tunsana, was charged with shooting in the head with a .45 pistol a 70-year old *Ata* called Matugol whom he accused of trying to wound his 20-year old daughter Leticia Saya, with a *surit-surit* in Ginubatan. Matugol had denied it, blaming his neighbour, Mangguan, for dropping the weapon outside his house."

Determined to make the best of his day off, Jack packed his compass and quadrant and set off by local bus, the beginning journey slowed by oncoming foot travellers waving at the already full bus, trying to make it stop.

"Steer round them, keep going -" a man at the front of the bus shouted.

"What's happening?" Jack asked his neighbour as families coming towards them clutching bundles and buckets beat on the windows. "Where're they from?"

"They're going to town," the man replied. "Keep going!" he shouted at the driver.

"We should stop."

"They might attack us."

"I'm a priest. I -"

The bus sped past.

Pushing to the front, shouting the bus to a stop, Jack got down at the beach turn-off and began to walk, the sea air clean and fresh after the packed bus, spiced with fragrance from flowers lacing the foliage. He cut through a band of trees to reach the beach. Up ahead he could see Norma, surrounded by people. Suddenly she saw him. Her face froze. Leaving the group she crossed to him.

"You mustn't come here!"

"I've every right to."

"I was followed last night," she glowered. "At a distance. When I turned down the beach road it went straight on. But coming back it was waiting and tailed me home."

"Why do you think they were following you? Who?"

Norma shrugged. "Keeping track. They knew where I was going: the beach road's a dead end. If the lights of the vehicle had been close together and high up I'd've been terrified. That'd be an army jeep."

Jack handed her the tape.

"!Can't you stick to the original plan? I suppose you came here on the bus?"

"Yes."

"And everyone saw you get off?" Norma rolled her eyes.

"This isn't about me! I want to ask a favour. Will you drive me out into the country when you're done here?"

Norma shook her head.

"The *country*?"

"Whatever you call outside town. Will you take me or not?"

Driving along the quiet road later calmed Norma.

"What is this about?"

"That woman who came to your house on my first day, remember?"

"Remember? I pass her walking this road every time I drive out here! You could set your watch by her!"

"Where does she go?"

"To my mother's shrine!"

"That's miles away!"

"What else has she to do? If she weren't such a - a – *peasant* – she'd make an ideal courier!"

Jack spread his map on his knee. "I want to look for her grandchildren. See here - "

Norma pulled off the road, turned the map towards herself.

"This is a good map."

"Church map."

"Better than government maps."

"Missionaries have different interests from governments. I've divided it into three. I want to browse *this* area -"

"There's nothing there! Nothing at all."

"Humour me."

"Take my word for it."

"These are tracks Norma. These dotted lines. Look."

"Well in *that* case," Norma stopped the car. "I need to approach from a different direction."

She did a loud three-point turn. They drove in companionable silence. Norma turned the radio on. After a while she pulled off the road, leaving the car concealed. They got out and stepped into the rainforest.

"It's quiet here -"

"That's a path. Come on, let's go." In dim light, hemmed in by foliage, they moved forward.

"See that - " Norma pointed at a tree fern's dense stem.

"We chop sections off those and plant things in them. Like plant pots. They hold the moisture."

Sweat dripped inside Jack's shirt. "I don't see how children could run through this." He looked around. "It's almost dark." He looked upwards for light but between him and the sky stretched giant webs dotted with spiders. Plants grown from seeds dropped by birds hung from the crotches of trees and where his feet disturbed leaf mould, a powerful smell dense.

"Hurry up!" Norma called. "Animals make those little tracks. Don't follow them. Ttt. Should have brought a *parang*."

"Listen!" There was a sharp sound. "What's that?"

"Leaf falling."

It descended noisily. The heat was oppressive; the air moisture laden.

"I'll have to sit down."

"Keep moving. You'll be covered in ants."

They continued walking 'til the meagre track petered out. Jack scanned around. "I was hoping to line my compass up with the silhouette of the hills – get a map bearing. I can't even see out of this clearing!"

"Told you there was nothing here. "

"Then why the track?"

A sudden burst of noise made them spin.

"What was that?"

The returning silence overawed them.

"I *know* that sound - " Jack mused.

"Sounds travel a long way. Could be 8 miles away -"

The sound came again.

"It's a chain saw!"

Like an angry animal awakened from sleep, the dragging and dredging noise grew, the dirge of earth moving equipment cut with a chain saw's whine.

"That's illegal logging," Norma stated. "They never get caught. At night their trucks creep in and months later you find the wheel marks and tree stumps."

"That would explain the tracks -" Jack looked at Norma. "We'd better get back -"

Nearing town they slowed to overtake refugee families limping along with their belongings.

"Where are they *coming* from?"

"Wherever, they'll end up on my beach," Norma said sagely. "Poor souls."

"But *where -?*"

"They're Visayans. I'd say there's been a squabble between new settlers and the tribals. And I don't blame the *Ata*. Those Visayans are supposed to be Christian," Norma glanced at Jack. "But they tell themselves that if an *Ata* accepts some shoddy toy from their *sari sari* store or puts his thumb mark on a piece of paper, they have some right to their land." She surged past them. "And then one day it catches up with them."

Jack had stopped listening. "Listen Norma," he said. "I want you to help me interview Emerenciana. I want to go back again – with a better idea of where – "

"OK," Norma smiled.

"But I think that's the area."

Every time Victor passed women refugees on the road – and they were growing thicker by the day – he felt bad. What was happening was horrible but, let it be remembered, not one shot had been fired by *his* command. The killings had broken out because of unhealed sores, not because of *him*. When the time was right, he'd be involved in *stopping* it. OK. He'd fired into a man's thatch, tossed a weapon over a wall. Hadn't the English poet Milton said: "Nothing is good or bad but thinking makes it so?" Or was that Shakespeare? What was happening was a short-term measure and he must not let it get to him. Mercifully the common sentiment in Davao City was that 'those *Ata* fighting amongst themselves are making the place unsafe for *Visayans* to live in!' People spoke of 'Yet another of their typical bouts of ritual revenge killings: just a *pangayao* between different branches of the tribe.'

"Is that your view?" Ricky had asked him pointedly at dinner.

"It's what The Press think -"

"But you can't deny *Atas* have been attacking *Visayans,*" Efigenia insisted. "You should do something, Victor."

"It's not my problem."

"This is about a native weapon," Ricky explained, "belonging to someone's father which a second group got

144

hold of and used in a name blackening exercise to implicate a third group."

"Any excuse to drag out the old blood feuds -" Victor shrugged. "When I think of all that peace making, settling them, getting them to grow *ipil-ipil...*" He shook his head.

"Have them get to the bottom of this silly argument!" Efigenia continued. "Let them have the face-saving ceremonies they need to make peace; let them exchange food and gifts like they used to! I can't say I care much whether the Visayans go back. But it's too much them flooding into town!"

"But aren't they victims?"

"Yes Jorge but -

"Mrs. Marcos is a *Visayan.*"

"I know Guinaldo, but she isn't down here interfering with the *Atas*."

"It was the *Atas* who started it."

"Maybe," Ricky put in. "But it didn't take long for the *Visayans* to get involved."

"They don't trust the *Ata* because they dress differently and have different customs," Norma stated. "They're perfectly civilised."

"You call shooting and killing a 14 year old schoolboy on his way to school with *surit-surit* civilized" Victor asked.

"If I was a *Visayan I'd* have stayed," Guinaldo shouted. "And formed a Defence Unit!"

"A lot of the men *have* stayed. That's their homes, their smallholdings they're protecting."

Victor stood. "There's no point talking about it."

"Please do something Victor," Efigenia bleated. "At this rate the army'll be called in."

"I shouldn't think so."

"If they do come, it'll be worse for the *Ata*." Efigenia continued.

"Why should we help the *Ata*?" Jorge asked. "They're not Christian."

"Some are. Many are perfectly good Moslems."

"God loves us all equally whether we are Catholic or child molesters or Buddhists."

"Thank you Norma."

"*If* the army come," Efigenia repeated. "They'll pinch all their trophies. My sister's cousin- in-law said the 60th battalion returned from the *Kalingas* with their ceremonial gongs and pre-Spaniard earthenware jars! 10,000 pesos a jar and the gongs went for up to 8,000! Think of that!"

Shaking his head, Victor gathered the newspapers from beside Ricky's chair: "I'm not getting involved." He left the room. Norma followed.

"If you don't, *someone else* might."

Victor returned her steady look. He knew for a fact the NPA were not present in Mindanao.

"Why do you say that?"

She gave him a knowing look, savouring the moment.

Victor crossed to Ricky's Range Rover.

"Would you stop by the Mayor's office and ask him to come over here?"

Elbow on the car window, hand resting on the wheel, Ricky looked down at Victor.

"This business with the *Atas* is upsetting your mother -"

Jack and Norma sat on driftwood on the beach facing Emerenciana.

"Ask where she came from."

"I did. She's got no idea."

Jack drew a map of Mindanao on the sand.

"That doesn't mean a thing to her." Norma shook her head. "You could draw 5 shapes and ask which one is Mindanao or even Africa and she'd have no idea." She sketched a long coastline, put in a big 'X': "That's the shrine you walk to. This is the sea line. Here's the big city. And here – the market … When you came here … which way did you get here from?" she asked. "This side? Over here? This side?"

Emerenciana's fingers wandered about the sand. Suddenly she exclaimed: "From here!"

Norma disagreed the area.

"No. You mean *here,* where the fighting is -"

"No!"

The woman piled sand, shaping a mountain ridge. "Here!"

Norma tapped the flat central area. "Surely you mean here, with the *Visayans* and -"

"No!" the woman insisted, smacking the slopes. Here. Where the *Mansakan* people live on the ridges." She snatched up Norma's match box emptied out the matches and began implanting them on the mountain slope. Norma leaned back. The woman *had* to be wrong.

"She seems certain," Jack shrugged. "It'd be worth taking a look -"

Norma considered.

"There's nothing there. I can assure you. The road stops short of the slopes. A bus goes from here as far as Tagum but - Tagum? Tagum?" she asked Emerenciana. The woman shook her head.

"You see? She's never heard of it. You're wasting your time."

"Someone has to try. We'll go in on foot. Ask her if she wants to come."

Emerenciana shook her head violently.

Up at Mansion Salcedo the Mayor was becoming increasingly uncomfortable.

"We can't have this going on our own doorstep." Victor shook his finger at the Mayor. "The Paquibato area. Don't you agree?"

"The problem – " the Mayor begun.

"The problem as *I* recall is that many *Atas* voted twice for you when you were elected. As did their children." The Mayor shifted on his seat. "It seems to me someone should at least have stopped the under twelves voting."

"Civil war-"

"On our doorstep is a disgrace. So get out there and see what you can do."

Victor watched the man leave. Though he hadn't at first seen it, the mayor was going to be very useful.

Jack's determination to give Emerenciana's missing grandchildren his best shot grew steadily. Here was a cause he could serve; here was practical activity. His concentration on one person's dilemma, he knew, struck Norma as odd but she hadn't baulked at sparing him a long bus journey followed by an even longer trek. Finally they arrived.

"This is Tagum!"

She pulled the car into a pot-pitted bus yard, battered wrecks panting around them, grinding up dust.

Sweltering women squatted under awnings by empty beer crates, half -heartedly selling coke bottles filled with home pressed oil while men in dusty pants ambled past them or leant against food shacks watching each other light cigarettes.

"What a place!"

"Come on." Norma led the way to a fly infested café where none of the food was really hot or the drinks cold. "Two colas please." They drank them warm to the rattle of a thin cat trying to pry dried food from a tin plate on the floor. Norma tapped the second quadrant on Jack's map. "I can drive a little way. You do know she said this was not the area? And I believe her."

"I intend to do all the areas."

Norma rolled her eyes.

Finding a track leading from the road, Norma drove along it for some way before parking up. "This'll have to do." She pulled a *parang* from under the seat, shook it about. "I'm not going further: it'll scratch the paintwork."

"Shall I carry that?"

"You wouldn't know how to use it."

They set off walking.

"You realise this is a complete waste of time?"

"Humour me."

"So this is the same area as last time but from a different side, right?"

"I hope so - "

The already intense heat beat down on them.

They picked a track leading into the hills.

"So those are the ridges where the *Mansakans* live?"

"Possibly. These are loggers track, where they've come back for giant trees they've marked out."

"Did you hear that? Like dynamite. There it is again!"

"That second one was an echo - "

Aiming at the sound, they left the track, Jack following Norma, plucking hooked leaves from his clothes as she slashed plants back, clearing a way.

"I hope we can find our way back - "

"Don't worry. Loggers tracks crisscross these areas. We'll be alright -"

Led by occasional bursts of sound, they went farther and farther into the forest, blundering into stilt roots, righting themselves; moss dropping into their hair, vines tripping them. Suddenly Norma stopped.

"Sssh!" She squinted ahead. The tree cover was thinning. There was a band of light.

"What is it?" Jack whispered, picking bark from his eyes. "A river?"

"Don't be stupid." They crept forward 'til they reached a sudden break in the cover. Before them lay a manmade ditch of clear orange earth

"It's a drainage trench."

They scanned ahead.

"For a road!"

"This is incredible!"

Jack stared at the wide, perfectly graded earth road, brilliant orange against the deep green jungle. Not a single track marked its surface. He looked at his watch.

"But Emerenciana knew nothing of a road – " Norma reasoned.

"It must go somewhere -"

"And she hadn't fled towards the rising sun: that's east - she'd never heard of Tagum - "

"You're saying we're in the wrong place - "

"Whatever this is, her grandchildren aren't here and we must be getting back."

"But let's have a look –"

Giving in, Jack pulled Norma out of the trench onto the road, their feet sinking into the sliding earth. Norma shook her head. "My father's roads aren't half this wide and they take refrigerated trucks - " She looked at her watch. "How quiet it is here."

Reaching a bend in the road, they peered ahead. To their amazement, the road ended almost as abruptly as it had begun.

"! It starts there and finishes up there. What's the point?"

"Something's coming!" Norma panicked. Near them an engine had coughed to life: they could hear the throaty noise of an approaching vehicle rattling towards them. They jumped back into the drainage trench.

"Look at our footprints!"

"Ssshh."

Slowly a jeep trawled past, INP on its side. Norma paled. "What's INP?" Jack asked.

"Integrated National Police – militarised - like your National Guard -"

"We don't have a National Guard. That's the Americans."

"Sort of Army -"

"Sssh. It's coming back."

The jeep returned past them, vanished round the corner. Unable to retrace their steps, they moved forward in the trench.

"Invest with Marcos and Marcos," Norma quipped. "Free military patrol with your first order!"

"For *road* building?"

"Someone might not want the road!"

"Would this be a private or public road?"

"Same difference. When private investment is government sanctioned, all installations become military!"

Up ahead a military gate with sentry box blocked the road.

"Good Lord!"

Beyond it, bright earth moving caterpillars rested in dips and craters in a scooped and pockmarked hill.

"Why the sentry box?"

"Sssh!"

Jack stared again at the road beyond the gate. "They're not doing a very good job," he observed. "They can't be using a theodolite."

"Let's get a little closer!"

"Isn't that dangerous?"

"Yes."

From the ditch, they watched a group of labourers, safety helmets to one side, sitting in the shade playing cards. A player got up and crossed to a belt of felled trees. Something was thrashing amongst the leaves. The man bent, pulled a creature up in one hand, slammed its head against a tree, threw it back down and returned to the card game.

"Is that an animal?"

"A *colugo*. They'll eat it tonight."

"Why not kill it properly?"

"No fridge."

The creature, which resembled a rat wrapped in a shawl, was trying to remove itself from the men's presence, to roll across the naked orange earth to the green canopy towering 150 foot above it.

"*Colugos* glide from tree to tree. They never come down to the forest floor. Once down they can't get up."
The helpless creature tried to flop itself away. Jack looked again at his watch.

"Norma – we must go -"

"Wait -"

The game had stopped at a dispute amongst the men. One of the men walked towards the *colugo* offering a pole which it, thinking it a branch grasped and held onto with both paws as the man lifted it in the air, it's head falling on one side, the furry membranes which would have borne it on the air, limp as sacking. He flicked it off towards their table, laughed.

"Don't look so sad Jack. The same is happening to our tribal people...."

A soldier looked at his watch, stretched, walked around the front of an army jeep, lifted the hood. Called out something. Another fetched a can of water from the back, unscrewed the cap and placed it on the hood. Clink! He started pouring water into the radiator. Another, fidgeted with his thigh, walked to the roadside and standing directly opposite Jack and Norma urinated in the bushes. Tugging at his fly, he rejoined the others. The jeep drove off.

"They're patrolling. We can't go back."

Beyond the military gate, Norma and Jack climbed out of the drainage ditch.

"This is dangerous," Jack warned as Norma sunk knee deep in the soft earth. "They've no idea how to build roads! The gradient's wrong to get over the hill -"

"We have to –"

"Look at our footprints!"

"Don't slip! You'll get buried alive!"

153

The banked earth gave way to loose shale, hot to the touch, which slid away as they sought footholds.

"Take my hand."

"Sssh! Those men were armed!"

Reaching the top, they could see the brief orange scar dead ending in the hill was no more than a break in the trees.

"It'll be a landing strip," Norma observed.

"We have to get back - "

"It's too late. I'm sorry."

Jack frowned.

"We wouldn't find the car before dark. It'll be dark *very* soon. If we start back at dawn we'll miss the military patrols. I'm really sorry." Norma began to walk doggedly along the mountain ridge: "Hurry up Jack."

"Where are we going?"

It was *her* country, up to *her* to find shelter, Norma told herself, praying they would stumble on a village. Should have turned back at three o'clock. Stupid! She *must* see smoke rising before dark. There must be smoke rising! Jack followed on the narrow path, its blue hills chequered with bald patches where slash and burn agriculture had taken place. He felt free. Finally he caught up with Norma.

"I hope you don't think I planned this deliberately," she threw at him, now virtually running.

She had detected voices, which was a comfort as slash and burn plantations meant little; tribals often walking miles from their villages to tend gardens.

Finally, over the heads of silver *toi toi*, almost shrouded in mist, a smattering of huts appeared, their roofs thatched with dead leaves. Naked children sat on the ground, black pigs chasing between them. Norma paused.

"They'll think you're a priest."

"I *am*."

"Like the American Fathers that tried to befriend them."

She walked to the centre of the huts, opened one of her pockets. Grubby children came forward and began earnestly exploring her pockets. Leaning on the huts, *Mansakan* women, their ears and lips stretched, glanced indifferently at the visitors and re-entered their huts. It was getting dark. Norma pursued one of the women. Jack followed.

Inside the hut a crouched woman with wide toed feet and ignorant eyes was droning in a monotone, clearly a sort of song. Opposite an old man seated on the ground, leaning on the wall, lifted his loin cloth and turned his penis in his hands, picking things off the underside. Their mouths were red as if they'd been chewing betel. "Go behind the house and take off your underpants," Norma said, "Give them to the woman of the house."

Jack stepped behind the hut followed by a crowd of children and came upon a squatting elderly crone, trying to beat off a pig that was pushing her into her own defecation. "Get away!" she was screaming to the children's delight, smacking the pig on the nose and losing her balance.

Jack half folded his Y-fronts, presented them to the woman who stuck them between the rafter and the thatch, then shouted and left the hut followed by the old man and children.

"This is our place now."

"Could you talk to them?"

"A bit. They complained. Lowlanders have been up here asking thcm to go away."

"Why?"

"They've been told their hill is going to move!" She rolled her eyes. "I'm afraid there's nothing to eat. I can't ask. People eat very early."

Jack settled on the floor. Through a gap in the roof, he looked at the sky. He was hungry. A few feet away, Norma too was looking at the sky.

"The difference between us and tribals generally," she observed, "is that they don't wake up and expect to be provided with a living. Lowlanders – that's us – expect to get born, go to school and some organisation will provide us with work. Well, some of us. They are completely self sufficient but they're easily destroyed because their identity is tied to the place they inhabit."

Why, Jack asked himself, are women so loath to take themselves seriously when it makes them so much more attractive? He looked over at Norma, lying on her back on the hard floor: "Their God has usually created that particular place just for them and they mustn't leave it, you see. They mostly all have complicated beliefs about being buried in that place and enriching the soil and eating their ancestors. We'd better go to sleep."

"How did their Gods make a place just for them?"

Norma grinned: "The *Kalingans* live on sheer mountainsides of massive rice terraces made before recorded history by their God, Kabunyan, with giant sweeps of his – his -." She hesitated. *"Member."*

"I see."

"When the old men there are blind they still work their fields. They know each inch of their land as if it were their bodies. When they *defend* their land, we behave as

156

if they doing something unnatural. Because they are tribals." She turned over: "Goodnight Jack."

Jack listened to her breathing, got up, went to the door.

Outside it was dark and cold, the sky above spangled with brilliant stars. He came and lay down. Norma turned over.

"My parents will be beside themselves!"

Conscious of the closeness of her breath, Jack said nothing.

"They'll *kill* me!"

"What do you mean you can't do anything?" Victor boomed.

"Please keep your voice down!" The Mayor begged, looking anxiously at the clock and hoping to leave. "It's getting late. I must -"

"The *Atas* are quite civilised!"

"In Wigiwigi a group surrounded a young farmer. His throat was slashed -"

"An *Ata*?"

"A Visayan. The *Ata* had mistaken him for an INP policeman. Because the INP had taken a man not knowing he was a deaf mute -"

"A Visayan?"

"An *Ata* -"

"I believe you're deliberately complicating this!"

"- from his field because he'd seen them mauling the *Atas* who'd cut the Visayans throat."

"This *is* complicated -"

"They'd strung him from a tree. Frankly, Mr. Salcedo, it's not clear what's happening out there."

"So you admit it. Who is leading the *Atas*?"

The Mayor looked uncomfortable. "I suppose Joe Pilayao. Certainly Lagiwan." He hung his head.

"So one or both of them?"

The Mayor nodded.

"Or they could be against each other or together?"

"Both." The Mayor nodded.

"At present. And this may change?" Victor tutted though this was turning out better than he'd dared hope. "Fine situation!"

"The impression I get -"

"Yes?"

"Is that if the fighting goes on, the stronger group, that's Joe Pilayao's, will wipe out Lagiwan's. Unless we arm him. When we've – *had dealings* with them before – you'll remember, we've only made progress by offering to favour one leader against the other."

"Are you suggesting we favour one side? It's bad enough it's become factionalised!"

The Mayor looked troubled.

"I'm looking to you to settle this," Victor warned, rising from his chair. "And I don't want the military here."

"We could try PANAMIN: the Presidential Commission on Minorities," the mayor suggested lamely.

"And look as if we can't handle our own affairs?"

"They have experience of these situations."

"That's an idea. In fact a very good one. Why didn't I think of it?"

"Sometimes the most obvious eludes us," the Mayor offered, rising weak with relief from his chair.

Victor clapped him on the shoulder: "I should let the local paper know what you're doing if I were you. Most commendable."

"Of course." The Mayor edged towards the door.

"However," Victor said looking sternly at him. "I'm not done with you."

Efigenia was sitting up in bed when Victor entered. He milled about the bedroom.

"You were very late with the Mayor."

"The man's doing his best."

"I wish the papers would leave off about these atrocities. Reading about people having their throats cut -"

"Would you prefer a special on Filipino Cookery," Victor said savagely climbing into bed.

Efigenia looked hurt. "What's the matter?"

Victor pulled the covers over his head.

Chapter Nine

Poised to make the descent to the road Jack waited for Norma who had insisted on going back to give his singlet to a woman wrapped in a faded cloth. He shivered. In the small hours with sleep almost coming, a cockerel had started scratching, clucking thoughtfully under the raised floor of their hut. Finally it had wandered off. Blissful silence, then the cock, remembering its vocation had shrieked ear splitting joy from their roof top. More silence: then its claws scratching above, dislodged dead thatch onto a sleeping sow who'd staggered loudly to her feet, slammed into their wall and belched, upsetting her piglets who'd run screeching in circles, finally settling with their loudly snuffling mother who lay down with a grunt. A man in the next hut spoke. The cock crowed again. A woman spoke. Jack looked at his watch. Not yet 2.00 am. This talk of cocks crowing at dawn was baloney. He sat up and looked at Norma, curled in a ball. He began to doze. A woman shouted. There was the sound of something thrown. A dog howled. He tried to sleep. A child started speaking.

Now waiting for Norma, Jack considered. These people had no privacy, no secrets or deceits. A whole range of behaviours dependent on the existence of solid walls was unknown to them. They relieved themselves in full view of each other; smiled readily and if they didn't like something, they glared.

When they'd got up that morning, there being no water, washing had not occurred. But sharp eyed Norma had spotted their gourds and filled their canteen. She'd also asked for and received two sticks of roasted corn for their journey down. No smiles, no social pretensions. She'd said: "Can we have this for our journey?" And the woman had nodded.

"We'd better hurry," Norma said arriving. "The workers'll be back and the military escort."

Jack looked at his watch. 5.00am. The village slept and rose to the pattern of darkness.

Following Norma he began to descend in sliding jumps, riding the cold shale, the canteen striking it, making a tinny sound that reverberated loudly. When they stopped for breath, the sound of awakening wildlife was heady. Before them, the sun could be seen warming up the tropical forest, making it steam.

"Listen!"

There it was. The sound of a jeep.

Reaching the bottom of the hill they stood listening.

"Hurry Jack -"

"Wait a minute -"

Brushing earth from his chest, he looked back at the savaged hill. "Norma," he called.

"What?"

"Come here."

She crossed to him.

"This isn't a road that goes anywhere."

"I know - " She pulled at his arm. "We have to get out of here!"

"Remember how it looked from the top? This is the beginning of an open-cast mine."

"And I'm General MacArthur!" She pulled him down into the drainage trench. "Get down!"

The jeep appeared. When it had passed, Norma began slashing at a right angle away from the road, foliage springing back behind them. "Emerenciana would have known something about all this – if she'd come from here." She glanced back at Jack. "It's probably an airstrip. Cross this segment off your map."

By 6.00 am they had hit a good path which descended gently, grass growing over it. Jack checked his compass. It made for easy walking and was wide enough for a cart. They slowed. Some heavy item had been dragged over the grass. Jack's eye moved to a stand of tapering bamboos to the right waving against the sky, the vegetation leading to it crushed and broken. At its foot lay sixty and eighty foot lengths of green bamboos, just off the path as if someone would return for them.

"Look!"

Standing still they became conscious of the sound of running water and in high grass saw, dripping from the hillside, a spring which tipped water onto an aged yellow split bamboo, supported on wooden pylons. It vanished shoulder high into the grass, carrying the water away.

"It's a water carrying system!"

They shaded their eyes. Before them as the land dropped, the piped water could be seen descending, flashing over a distance of half a mile to a valley floor.

"There are certainly people living here!"

"Take a reading. We'll come back."

Reaching the car, Norma drove dangerously. "So frustrating! Just needed a few more hours!"

"Can you slow down?"

"I'm trying to think of an excuse – What's the time now?"

"I'd rather not tell you."

Once home, Efigenia caught her in the kitchen.

"I didn't hear you come in last night -"

"Didn't you?"

"They're still at it you know. Did you hear their raised voices?"

Norma cocked an ear. "Was the mayor here all night?"

"Till late. You did right not to disturb them. Your father's really worked up. That man's next to useless!"

Norma put her hand on her mother's arm.

"I'm sure things will work out."

"Do you really think so Norma?"

"I do."

"He's been here since before breakfast. I'd like to take them in a drink but -"

"I'll do it -"

Very excited at having gotten away with it, Norma busied herself making a tray of coffee.

She carried the tray in.

"Did you try PANAMIN?" her father was demanding of the Mayor.

"I've written and phoned."

Norma placed the tray down.

"You don't need to be in here Norma."

"Sorry."

Victor waited until she had left.

"And?"

"It will take time -"

"Then we must wait."

"But Pilayao has asked us to help him wipe out his enemy Lagiwan!"

"The man's a complete savage."

"He's offering to divide up all the land taken between the Davao River and Tibitibi between himself and *whoever helps him take it.*"

"He can forget that."

"He's offering to plant the land taken," the mayor inched nearer to Victor. "Not his half – with *falcatta* trees." He paused. "Which could be used to supply pulp for a carton factory."

Salcedo pressed his lips together. "I am not interested in the *falcatta* and don't expect you to be either." His voice sounded clipped. "*No side deals.* If I catch you trying to pass land to others…." He stood. "It'll get back to me. Then this'd be the last time you'd enjoy my patronage."

"Surely," the mayor stood. "If PANAMIN won't come, the lesser of two evils is to arm Pilayao? If you want the fighting stopped! Or call in the army?" He watched Victor.

"If you understood the *Atas* at all." Victor began icily. "You'd know they like someone to *win.* Then they re-establish on the basis of a peace pact -"

"Then we *must* arm one side -"

"I can't go along with that."

Feeling he was in an impossible position, the mayor lied:

"Pilayao said Lagiwan's lot were involving the *Atas* on your plantation." He began to feel frightened. Why wasn't the man negotiating? "Because in the last war before they retreated to your hills they had cut off the heads of some Lagiwan supporters and taken them there…"

"If my plantation is attacked," Victor said slowly, "I will defend it. As to the other matter, I am allowing you to settle it however you choose. Without, I repeat, the army. If you can't take care of a handful of squabbling natives, what good are you?"

With a bit of luck, thought Victor as the Mayor left, he'd go ahead and arm one side, get caught in threats and arm the other and in no time both sides would have hand grenades and rocket launchers. *Then* would be the time for the army to come and for PANAMIN to move quickly to usher the tribals to a place of safety. "Warring *Atas* Unite Against Military" the headlines would say. Followed by "Army Shoots Indiscriminately." Not bad!

Marabut handed Margolas a note: "Put this in tonight's edition of the Manila Press.

> 'The presence of the NPA has been reported in the strife torn Paquibato Area of Davao del Norte.'

"Is that true?"

"No. But useful."

"What about that Mayor wanting us to go down?"

"Victor's playing him. Write a Dear Mayor letter. We are saddened to hear of the renewal of disputes within your *barrio* but before intervening feel it essential that the parties be brought together and allowed to have peace talks. No one, including you, I am sure, would want outside intervention unless the *Atas* themselves requested it."

But the article re the NPA, repeated in the *Mindanao Journal,* sent the Mayor running to Victor.

"It's a mistake," Victor told him calmly. "Give a news conference. Say local business interests – which will be taken to be me – can confirm that the NPA are **not** here, regard this as a storm in a teacup and are against the involvement of the military. Say you are negotiating with both sides and expect an early resolution."

"But the NPA?"

"Rubbish! Make sure the article is under a large item on my new hospital. And keep this thing in proportion. Now get out!"

Furious, Victor strode up and down. How Marabut and Margolas could imagine the NPA item would help....! If they brought in the army now, the land would be cleared so fast Visayan settlers would be *back* and re-established before the UN Commission arrived to declare the land unoccupied!

The Mayor however saw it differently. Manila believed the *New People's Army* had come to Mindanao to support the *Ata* tribals. That meant Manila would send in the military and spare him the trouble. So the item had been an error? Soon put that right! He made for his favourite bar and waited for the INP chief to arrive: "Over here," he called. "I'll get this round."

"They hadn't even missed me!" Norma smiled as Jack climbed into her car. "We'll be there by lunchtime, back by tea!"

"Here." Jack slipped his recorded tape into her dashboard. "Whoever types this'll find something strange on the tape."

"What?"

"There's a complaint that men claiming to be NPA members are infiltrating *Ata* areas but a store keeper has recognised two of them as INP men."

"Hah!" Norma laughed. "That means one thing. The NPA *aren't* here. No one would *dare* impersonate them."

"There was a report in the Manila paper –"

"Look. If they *had* been here, Manila would have sent in the army. This is an attempt to militarize the situation and bring in the army to –"

"An *Ata* said the men posing as NPA are going round helping themselves to food and extorting money –"

"Where are we headed?"

Jack pulled out the map. "There is a depression here." He tapped the map. "I think it's the valley the water was descending to. By its position, I would say it's the place we almost saw."

"So which way -?"

"We can access it from the Tagum end, by track if we can find it, or blunder through bushes from the other side."

Norma looked at him. "Tagum it is!"

They drove in companionable silence.

Finding a track and parking the car as far up as possible, they started walking, ultimately emerging on a wide ridge covered with *paragrass.* Below them lay a spacious grassy bowl, with a lake, fields, orchards and a village spread around it.

"Look at that!"

The settlement stood mainly to one side of the lake, its wooden houses in rows and what looked like a meeting hall or school in the centre. The silence was ethereal. Only the sound of a hand saw reached them.

Quietly they descended to the houses, peeping around corners. On the balcony of the first house, a child dozed in a swing hammock, its arm hanging loose; from the balcony rails, orchids cascaded from slabs of tree fern.

"Hasn't been a massacre here!"

"Sssh."

A cock strutted past, moving its head cautiously, looking at them. It jumped up, displayed on the verandah, its claws making a scratching noise which half woke the child and beneath the hammock a dog opened its mouth, yawned. The cock fluttered onto a washing line. The hum of the surrounding foliage was loud.

"This place wasn't on the map."

"We'd better call out."

"Just a minute." Crossing to a sound of splashing water, Jack stared at dragon flies skimming a pool where the bamboo sluice they had seen ended.

"!Come look – This water's been carried all the way here by bamboo!"

"Don't let your husband stand in the sun!" a voice called. Norma spun round. A woman was standing on the balcony. "Come in!"

Inside, the hardwood floor was cool and smelled of beeswax. The floorboards, benches, beams – all were of single timber slabs, darkened with age, polished.

"What is this place?" Norma asked.

"New Cebu. After Cebu, where we came from." The woman smiled. "We are 70 families. You'll have seen our giant cabbages in Davao City market."

"I have!" Jack agreed.

"How did you come to be here?" Norma asked.

"The place had been abandoned. We heard. So we came here."

"Has anyone been here asking you to move?"

"Why would they?" The woman laughed. "We wouldn't move! We're too well established! And we're quiet as death."

Norma considered. "Do you know anything about a new road?"

"New road?" She repeated. "You go out *our* track and you get the bus and you'll be in Davao tonight."

"From Tagum?"

"Tagum? Don't know Tagum. We have our own track. We made it from the trunk route we came walking down. Here comes my husband. Look what I've found!" She shouted.

Dropping his bundles on the balcony, a man in torn pants, bare feet and scratched legs advanced offering his hand:

"I'm Joma! Ida's husband!"

"Norma. Jack."

"Show them around while I get lunch Joma!"

"Let me put on a clean shirt!"

"They must know about Tagum," Norma whispered. "Don't tell me they've never explored that track -"

"If they're trespassing maybe they wouldn't want to be seen emerging that way too often -"

"Then they're exiting through your last quadrant - "

Joma reappeared in a patched shirt. "This way!" He skipped down the steps like a young man. "This place was a two and a half hour hike from the road when we came here," he said leading them towards the lake. "If we crossed the Lumangang Creek once we crossed it eighteen times! And the Masara River! But we've carved a track out now. Six kilometres and good enough for a *carabao* cart.*"

"That'll be the track we saw – " Norma whispered. "Last time."

"Over there," Joma called pointing across the lake. "That smoking rock is a volcano. We stocked this lake ourselves: *tilapia* fish, *hito*, *dalag*. It had eels," he continued. "We grow papayas, pomelos, guavas, lemons, jack fruit, squash, beans, corn – "

169

"Life is good, eh?"

For answer he indicated a pig, asleep with her head in the slop bucket.

"When I am an old man I shall sit back, my fruit trees grown tall!" He grasped a cricket and crammed it in his mouth. "We worked hard but we're secure now." One of the cricket's legs stuck out. "Coffee hills only need 5 months attention a year at harvest." He crunched the cricket loudly. "When we came we only planted *gabi* and *camote*, for the pigs. And corn. At first. We come from barren land you see. We had no experience of growing potatoes or cabbage. But we found accidentally a head of Shanghai cabbage could yield 5 kilos if you fed it milk, and cauliflower bulbs could go a kilo and a half -"

"Do you have title to the land?" Norma asked delicately.

"We kept quiet about being here," Joma said lowering his voice. "It belonged to a foreigner once. But the land had long lain idle…. We put in for title. It's allowed. But we heard nothing. But no one came to throw us off." He turned back towards the house. "The height of the valley makes for a cool climate which is why our vegetables can compete."

"Did you apply for title more than once?"

"Many times! All of us! We paid a lawyer and we applied! But we heard nothing! We're saving up money to put towards the government sending us a teacher! We'll apply!" He pointed to the name above the school. "New Cebu. You see? The "New" means our hope. We've built a teacher's house. In the evenings this area is blanketed with white fog because of the humidity. You get a good night's sleep."

"Has there been any violence in the area?" Jack asked. "Any reports of soldiers?"

"Soldiers?" the man asked. "Not even the tax man comes here!" He became serious. "There is one little mystery though -"

"Lunch! Lunch!" Ida was calling as children came running towards the house.

"This way!" Joma ushered them in.

"You sit at the head," Ida patted Jack's arm, placing Norma beside him and asking. "Where did you meet your American husband?"

"Actually -" Norma began.

"You must come often!" Ida interrupted, stretching towards a dish. "When we have been recognised as a town, our name will be on the map! Grace!"

The family bowed their heads in prayer. As soon as it was appropriate, Jack urged:

"Tell us your mystery - "

The mood became solemn. Ida looked around the table. The child nearest Norma rose: "Shall I get them?" Ida nodded. Through the door they saw her run to another house, heard her voice coaxing. "Come…. It's alright... Come ..." All eyes were on the doorway as they heard feet moving unwillingly towards them, scuffling closer. "It's alright. Come …" The child backed into the room pulling the wrist of a boy of 7 or so clasping an infant. Norma drew breath.

"These two – and an older girl who was dying of snake bite – arrived on the edge of our village one evening," Ida explained. "Her leg was swollen like a pillow. What it must have cost her to walk!" Her eyes filled with tears. "Before she – went unconscious – she told this one," she indicated the 7 year old boy. "Tell them this, tell them that. Which we do not understand why she said because this child is entirely dumb."

Norma looked at the 7-year old, his features vaguely familiar. "Perhaps she was delirious."

"He has not uttered *one word*," Ida insisted, "since they arrived. If he has nightmares, the bed rattles. Why was he told tell us this and that?" she demanded, "if he can't talk?"

"We called the baby Lolita," a child said, reaching to take her but the little boy clung on fiercely. "She looked about 8 months."

"We cut the bite and sucked," Joma explained. "It was too late."

"Their feet were *pitted* with thorns as if they'd been paid to jump in them," Ida added. "Their clothes were in *ribbons*."

"This boy could cry," Joma added. "Though he was fevered. He cried tears like I have never seen from a child."

Norma looked at the glazed eyes of the 7-year old before her.

"I think we know where their grandmother is," she said breathlessly. "Could you bring the children to Davao?"

"The woman that cares for them is in Davao today. That boy won't go anywhere without her. He won't go with another."

"I'll try and bring the grandmother here - "

"Come back when the woman is here. They'll go there with her -"

Norma hesitated: "The grandmother lives in a beach community. You wouldn't find it. On Fridays she goes to the city market. You know the market don't you? She waits for another grandchild who's in service."

Ida nodded. "I'll tell them. Sometimes people from here go in on a Friday."

"Will you tell Emerenciana about it or hope they come to town or what?" Jack asked as they drove back.

"I don't want to raise her hopes - " Norma's eyes shone.

"We may be near where she fled from!"

"But two children - one mute? She's looking for four -"
After twenty minutes of thoughtful silence, Norma asked:

"Why did you become a priest?"

"I was seeking."

"And have you found?"

"Not yet."

"Will you go home?"
Jack shook his head. "You can't ask how it will pan out. A call comes. You answer it."
Norma stared from the window. "You'd've made a good father."

"I hope to!"

"I don't know what will happen to me."

Back home unable to sleep Jack reached down his map and compass. However unlikely Norma had thought his idea about an open cast mine had been, he'd seen one near the seminary in Yorkshire and it was not unlike what they'd seen from that hill top on the previous trip: a pit of dug earth with mounds of loose earth and tracks winding between them. He opened the map and studied the chain of hills. There was probably no connection but if he was right in his calculations - he checked the scale of the map – the populated valley of New Cebu was separated by a distance of 7 kilometres from the disturbed earth. Or 4.34 miles as the crow flew.

Victor climbed into his pickup and hit the gas. You couldn't keep a Salcedo down. Nothing, he congratulated himself, outwardly indicated that things had changed. Fredo, with his patience for experimental work, was overseeing the two new banana strains that had arrived in temperature-controlled crates: the one to be grown alone, the other crossed with their own produce and hand pollinated. The polythene sheaths too had arrived, their rustle adding a new sound to the banana groves and, with 8 team leaders, Ricky had combed the plantation, saving up to 20% of the immature fruit. The 'pesticide spoiled' crop had been taken care of, directed to Manila and paid for on arrival at the price he'd invoiced PANAMIN – the exact sum he would have got from *Del Mundo*. The hospital was going ahead. Things were on course. But what if...? That question haunted him. What if the *Ata* made peace and returned to their land? Or the army came too soon and cleared the area allowing it to be re-colonised by November 1st? Or a Commander in the INP acquired so much land he felt the need to *defend* it and struck a deal with the army? Or what if he *didn't* clear the area or cleared it with some scandal so the mine venture cried off? *Focus*, he told himself. Get on top of the Press. Weed out problems.

First, the wrong kind of local publicity could attract the Moslems of Zamboanga – within reach and always ready for a scuffle. Their *Moro National Liberation Front* could try to incorporate the Paquibato area into *their* secessionist claim, which would draw international attention to *their* longstanding war with Manila so that

174

any gain to him could be forgotten! He parked up outside the newspaper office and went in.

"By using the word *datu*," Victor said aggressively to the editor. "You are raising this tribal squabble to an inappropriate level! It's an Islamic word belonging properly to the Sulu Archipelago. To speak of *datus* in Mindanao meeting and agreeing, gives the whole issue unwarranted dignity. What's wrong with 'headman'?"
The editor shrugged.

"You seem to think that because you are dealing with *Atas*, not the military, you can say what you like. You should quieten down until things blow over."

"Did you object to our reporting that an INP man who had posed as an NPA member had been found buried in a shallow ditch the next day?" the editor asked, leaning back in his chair.

"Not if it was true. Of course not! But to suggest, as you did in a previous article, that arms and literature found on a murder victim indicated he was a genuine member of the NPA was patent nonsense! Are they posing as NPA or are they NPA? Make up your mind."

"I'm unbiased."

"To mention the ages of children killed makes bad reading."
The editor said nothing, thereby making his point. Then he leaned forward: "So you think things will blow over?"

"Or be resolved. Of course. Provided you don't inflame them. Which would raise questions about your fitness to operate, your responsibilities as an editor notwithstanding.

He walked angrily to his pickup. If the man knew half of what he knew he'd be saving his steam for the finale!

175

Yes, people were on the move. Like a mad board game 3 families running to Panabo had become 10 families running to Santo Tomas, causing 5 families to flee to Paradise Embak, displacing 10 families who'd fled to Pandaitan, then 50 families to Tibitibi! Unstoppable. Malakibo and Labok in Tapak had been evacuated. Kimananaw and Mapula... They were even fleeing places they had evacuated to! Which, on the face of it, was very good. Well done him! Away from Apalili and back to Salapawan and Agsam! But *what if....* In the market, it was common knowledge that Kinse-Kinse, Montiflor and Mekulot were deserted. 300 families had now left Panabo and Santo Tomas; the population of Pigdalahan had shrunk from 332 to 52 persons and this was only the beginning. Not bad for an evening's walk with a *surit-surit*. But he must stay on top, hold the reins tight like a Roman charioteer controlling a team of horses. You could not stop people talking, no, but you could keep the whip handy!

"I hear the *Ata* have opened a third front," Efigenia said brightly as he returned home.

"That is because our neighbour, with his eye on the *falcatta* land, is backing Pilayao's private army."

"How would that start a third front?"

"The dud mayor has encouraged a third *Ata* to stage an uprising against Pilayao to 'prove his strength and leadership,'" Victor said patiently. "And promised him political favours and relief goods in exchange for 'loyalty' in forthcoming elections..." He looked at her. She had not understood. He sighed. "People are always ready to capitalise on disorder."

"There is a lot for you to worry about Victor -" she consoled. "Don't take it personally."

"I don't like to see people manipulating these ignorant *Atas.*"

"I know."

He sat tiredly. There was no point in praying. Not 'til it was over.

Efigenia spoke again. "I know our current Mayor, is being criticized -"

"Only by the dud mayor."

"For not giving the *Ata* schools, medicines, roads -"

"None of it matters," Victor stood "I'm going to lie down."

"To say it doesn't matter is very harsh!" Efigenia called after him.

"I mean," he turned. "In the present climate, he would be criticized whether he had done it or not." Actually, all that mattered was that the land was cleared. At the right time. But Efigenia, who felt Victor was missing a trick though what she did not know, would not let it go. As they were turning in that night, she murmured: "I hear Lieut. Callada's letting *Atas* eat free in his plantation canteen."

"Only because he's got his eye on a cacao project," Victor said tiredly. "Go to sleep Efigenia, none of it matters. Go to sleep…."

"Any day now," Marabut stated. "People will ask why we don't intervene -"

"Good."

He passed the newspaper over.

"Visayans and natives both," Margolas read, "have been forbidden by the PC/INP to go to their fields to get food. 9 died of hunger and sickness in Migkawayan, 6 in Amutag -"

"Oh shame."

"- caught in the conflict between Pilayao and Lagiwan's forces others are kept on the move and unable to bury their dead -"

"Pilayao and Lagiwan at each other's throats. Check."

"- Joel Manlangan, Kaabag of Kinse-Kinse reports many *Ata* are sick and hungry there and in Salapawan -"

"We could go in now."

"Let me finish – '… further complain that the INP and Local 59th battalion shoot any *Ata* they find in outlying areas like Kinaw-anan. The ones arrested had asked and gotten permission to go and work in their fields but were arrested there."

"I don't want the 59th getting too powerful -"

"Three *Atas* killed by Visayan CHDF members were alleged to have ambushed Fidel Mangco, aged 25, when he went to cut wood at the river bank. He was shot and wounded by surit-surit at 5.00 a.m." Margolas chuckled.

"Surit-surit! Who but an *Ata?"* He laid the paper down.

Marbabut counted off on his fingers. "People dying of malaria and sickness. Lack of food. They can't plant corn or rice for next year because of the fighting and land in the other areas is already planted to *ipil-ipil*. They can't return to their lands. They're on the move. So it's time to move."

"Not by Victor's reckoning -"

"Aha! But Victor doesn't know!"

Marabut pulled out a notepad: "So what will you tell him? Because if we move in, he'll -"

"We don't give Victor reasons!"

"He'll ask!"

"OK. One, tell him we don't like church involvement. It's bound to be there: no need to prove it. Two, say we're only *establishing* safe havens for the *Ata*. They don't have to use them. And three -" his eyes searched the ceiling.

"We're prepared to back off if he doesn't like it."

"As if."

"So put on your hail-fellow-well-met voice and get on that phone."

"Victor!" Margolas purred. "You've done well. However we're coming in now." He felt the shock hit Victor. "All we have in mind is the *delineation* of a couple of special *Ata* settlements – in, say, Tibitibi and Simod, where the two factions – there *are* still only two factions I take it (?) – could retreat to. We'll give Lagiwan and Pilayao special PANAMIN titles to encourage cooperation. And, of course, privileges." Victor listened. Should he tell them it wouldn't work? Because Moslem *Ata datus* regarded Pilayao and Lagiwan as common thieves and would never retreat into centres with them. Plus the *datus* followers would stay out with them. Should he point that out?

"You're quiet Victor," Margolas waited.

"I have confidence in your judgement," Victor heard himself saying cordially. After all, as long as his debts were taken care of. But would they be if the thing fell apart before November 1st? Which, at this rate, it would.

"It is always pleasant to speak with you," Margolas smarmed, "And to enjoy your good will."

"I am happy with everything," Victor replied.

He was, in fact, *furious*, he realised, catching sight of his reflection in the picture of the Sacred Heart. Even if Pilayao and Lagiwan and their henchmen retreated to the settlements in return for bribes, the continued occupation of the area by the *datus,* the Christian Visayans and others would be seen as 'resistance' to a peace plan: the army would then move in to clear the area and genuine slaughter would follow. The Moslem press would be straight onto it. International headlines of the exact sort they had told him to avoid. And why? *When he had achieved everything without an outside shot being fired.* They were taking things out of his hands *on his territory,* trying to make *him* fit in with their inferior assessment of the situation. Very well! He would unleash the next layer and show them just how inappropriate the establishment of the safe havens at this time was!

Eleven at night. The Grundig hummed quietly as Jack tried to sort the notes into some kind of order. Two PC soldiers and three *Ata* killed in Agsam. Where was Agsam? A writer complained that the newspaper would not take a story from her. Probably she wouldn't give them her name. Maybe she'd wanted money? *Maybe it hadn't happened.* He yawned. One person killed in an ambush at kilometre 28; a logging vehicle ambushed in Malabog and an *Ata* named Fermin was being used by a Lieutenant Arana of the INP who owned a coffee plantation near Malabog and employed ex-convicts and wanted men for very low salaries. Was this two items on one note or were loggers trespassing on land marked out by a member of the military for the expansion of an existing coffee plantation? He yawned. Or was *he* being used? About to slip the notes back into a folder and give up, he heard a noise. He moved to the door. Someone was there. He sprung the door in the face of the sacristan.

"What do you want?"

"You were talking. I thought someone was with you -"

"Knock!"

The sacristan held up the door keys, trying to peer around him.

"I came to set your breakfast things. The housekeeper will not be in tomorrow -"

"Thank you. I can do it myself."

He waited 'til the man had gone.

"Catholic Father," the next note begun. "We Moslems and despair of State help turn to you make our plight known." It was written on lined paper from an exercise book. "We four *datus*," they named themselves, "have complain to Lieut. Arana because son of Ongkay is taken hostage by INP for no reason. And he take Ongkay hostage for complaining and keep him until Ongkay other son surrender because he say other son give land to loggers." Logging trade, *datus*...? He read on. Objecting to this treatment, the three remaining *datus* had complained to the Mayor who had accused them of having links with subversives and of thievery. Maybe the person who typed the Detainee Situationers could make sense of it! "*Datus* complain of victimization," he begun, still reading ahead. "Inside he box us (punch us about), take a lot of money our relatives bring before release..." the note went on. Jack rubbed his eyes. They wanted to accuse the council secretary, Toto, of working hand in hand with the local 59th PC battalion... He yawned. The remaining unsigned notes stated the *datus* were good men and the charges against them fabricated. Managing to summarise it, Jack was about to switch the Grundig off when he remembered something. It was his duty to convey information: not to understand it. And didn't *he* have some information himself? He pulled the Grundig closer to him. "A reliable source," he began, so softly the Grundig's hum almost covered his words. "Indicates that mining operations may be about to begin in an area which has been cleared with brutality to the north of Davao city at an approximate compass reading…" he paused and switched off the Grundig. There it was again, the sound as if his outer door had been left open.

In his study, Victor arranged and re-arranged three pieces of paper: The *Datus*. The Logging. The Church. This would be a harder fuse to set, but done properly, would keep the show under wraps 'til 1st November. He rose to get a drink. If Manila thought he'd played his best card, they were in for an awakening.

Chapter Ten

"The English priest," people nodded as Jack passed. Shopkeepers called greetings, a stallholder broke an orange for him to try. Someone was following him. He'd known since the night he'd been interrupted dictating, but the feeling was light. These days the sense of a barrier between himself and the people had been lifted to be replaced with an awareness that there were things they knew that he should not be told. His attitude to them too had changed as he shared risks that were a part of their lives. He felt more sure of his vocation, his Englishness, the very mix of who he was. It was almost as if, before his involvement in the Detainee Situationer, while saying Mass, he had not picked up on nuances in the congregation. His prayers had been detached: something they listened to. Now he sensed they could feel him feeling their difficulties, the stumbling blocks desperation had placed in their way. He felt less guilty as a Westerner, coming before them with ostensibly clean hands but from a strong country, and even the women's suffocating femininity washed past him now as he saw it was about power, not principle. Except Norma. They withheld because they were poor: had few bargaining chips. To stay strong as a person, to fulfil his ministry, there was much to understand.

Crossing the square he watched the crowd flowing towards the Cathedral laughing, chattering, the men's hair oiled, the women bright as peacocks. Show time. The nine o'clock Sunday Mass when people came together with goodwill, saw each other at their best. Safely. *The* social event of the week, no ticket needed. Community, after family, was the basis of society and he was there to encourage them in their pursuit of Christian precepts. So how seriously did they take him? Was it possible the Church, and he himself, were no more than a halfway house, a pre-lunch convenience? He had made a gift of his life to them, but did they take his words seriously? And did *he* mean them? Or was he irritable because he was hungry?

"Father!" A voice called. He turned. The woman, Emerenciana, was there, holding the hand of a child. "My daughter Wilma." The child bobbed a sort of curtsey.

"Hello Wilma," Jack smiled.

"Today is a feast day. Her family are over there -" Emerenciana nodded at a local family.

"Do you have any news?" she persisted.

Jack reached for her arm. Was it safe to be seen talking to her? "This is not the place to talk. Talk to Miss Norma at the beach." She crossed herself, hurried into the cathedral. Jack continued greeting parishioners as they mounted the steps, then went to vest. For some reason he felt irritable.

"Ready, Father," an altar boy said, leaning from the vesting room to ring the bell. Jack glanced out. All there. The owner of the Marakesh Hotel and the Apa Golf and Country Club. Lieutenant Arana, rumoured by the notes to have a coffee plantation on *Ata* land. And there was the agent for Philippine Airlines who'd winked at him at a wedding, and said to be remembered if he needed anything – sitting with his cousin, who ran the Ministry of Tourism – despite the fact that Mindanao was officially closed to tourists. And wasn't that the Principal of Davao City High School hovering in conversation with the Director of the University of Southeastern Philippines

College of Engineering...? Jack straightened his chasuble. Both mayors would be somewhere. Sitting apart. He could make out the leaders of Cleaning Teams A and B – they always arrived early - squeezed into the same bench as the Post Office counter clerk, now past the age of marriage but still looking and clearly not interested in the near relative of the Cleaning Team B leader....

He peered through the door jamb, his collar itching. Why not? If anyone needed telling it was the Commander of the 59th battalion, lingering in civvies, his mother on his arm, waiting to be let into a bench by the sacristan, too busy keeping an eye on a man who had spoken of starting an Opposition party, to realise he was bench blocking. There they were, through the door jamb, this collection of chatting humanity, come for their weekly salve! Apart from Emerenciana, these were not the dispossessed: they were the soldiers, the members of CHDF's, the people who ate.

Following the procession he moved onto the sanctuary. In the front row were the Salcedos, including Norma who had said the government had to be fought because it was corrupt. She looked away. It was her friends who typed his notes, met in secret places like early Christians. What crazy game was this country playing, telling tales to the Church, trying to make their peace with God over a couple of beers and a "You see, father, things being the way they are...?" His stomach rumbled. They hired themselves out as killers, took bribes, went to lengths to cheat tribals of their ancestral lands; used *him* to reinforce the social fabric of their existence with convenient scales of guilt and reward, then appeared at the confessional with smoking guns expecting him to make an accommodation with God!

He moved into the Mass. Time to put the record straight. The *Confiteor* came, Victor along with everyone else, striking his breast. If he *was* fingered as the local link for the Detainee Situationers, they'd get rid of him without a second thought! The *Kyrie* came, Efigenia and all the children asking the Lord to have mercy on them, Christ to forgive them. He'd raised Emerenciana's hopes. She'd lost children, grandchildren. The first readings, done by youngsters, passed. A woman read the responsorial psalm: the congregation answering clearly: "Taste and see that the Lord is good!" Norma had not believed about the mine because she had never seen one. The Gospel came. Jack kissed the Bible. These people wanted him to justify their behaviour. They had no intention of taking what he said seriously. He read the marked section, kissed the book again, raised it above his head and held it to the congregation. "This is the Word of the Lord," he announced. "Thanks be to God," they chirped. Now or never!

"When we say the Our Father," Jack began. People settled back on their benches, the women taking out handkerchiefs and fans. "We say 'Thy Kingdom come'. That means we want God's kingdom to come on earth and are willing to work towards that end." The political candidate cracked his knuckles. "We say Give us this day our daily bread. Not Give us a mineral deposit and help us drive away the folk who live on it," he continued, "so that we may accumulate not just our daily bread but enough for the rest of our lives." Victor blanched. Jack caught the look in Norma's eyes that said he was going too far. "On earth
as it is in Heaven?" He looked around. "What barriers exist in Heaven between man and man?" Efigenia slipped

186

an arm through Victor's. "We are told, they that mourn will be comforted: they that hunger and thirst for justice will have their fill: that in fact the Kingdom of Heaven is available to the poor in spirit and that it is harder for a man tied to his wealth to enter Heaven than for a camel to climb through the eye of a needle." Norma was shaking her head at him. "We have to decide whether to follow the ways of the world or God's way," Jack summed up. "As the dying Joshua told his people: 'Choose whom you will follow.' "

As the congregation rose for the Creed he felt the massive silence.

"They'll think you're a communist!" Norma hissed after Mass. "You won't be any use!"

"I'm a priest."

People hung back afraid to approach him.

"I thought that a fine sermon," Victor said loudly. "Congratulations."

"Your voice carries well," Efigenia agreed. "Clear diction."

"It wasn't a personal attack."

People began to draw near.

"My dear boy," Victor assured him. "We were proud of you!" He climbed into his car. The whole thing was unravelling before his very eyes. He drove in silence. Out on the open road, he turned to Efigenia: "Who built that Cathedral?"

"He's just a young boy. He needs our support."

"I'll tell you what support *I* have in mind -"

"The children are very fond of him."

"There's one place that boy'll get all the chance he wants to preach the gospel!"

187

"That *priest,* Victor."

"How *dare* he insult the congregation? They'll stop putting money in the plate!"

"Then the Church will support him."

"Only as long as people put money in plates."

"His parents can send money. You're overwrought."

"Boys like that – their parents have pensions – invested in Unit Trusts -"

"It was his *first* major sermon -"

"What do you think those Trust's portfolios bulge with? Not soft commodities like bananas. Minerals! Like he was complaining about! That's where the foreign investment comes from!"

"He didn't mention bananas."

"Exactly!"

"Then why so touchy?"

"Why attack minerals?"

"Because nobody has any!"

Victor decided to shut up.

"You're getting very sensitive," Efigenia observed. "I'd like you to see a doctor."

"!Leave me alone!"

Bruised by the encounter, Efigenia made for her shrine, sat staring into the dark. "You saw that God. What am I supposed to do?" She felt like crying. Behind her the psst psst of the woman who was always there reached her.

"You have answered my prayer!" Emerenciana exclaimed to the statue. "I feel it in my heart! Oh I trust you! I will speak to the lady at the beach. When she comes. I'll ask her...."

Efigenia looked at the woman's bowed head. "Lord," she prayed. "Hear my sister's prayers. Our circumstances are different but … You said that where two or more are gathered in your name, there you are in the midst! Grant her petition." She rose. It would be shoddy to add 'grant it so that my shrine will get its miracle and be officially recognised.'

The woman too had risen and was coming towards her. How could she look so happy?

"Señora," Emerenciana began. "I pray for your intentions every day. God bless you."

Ricky knocked and entered. His father glared.

"Is it true about the mineral deposit?"

"Who knows?"

He looked shrewdly at Victor.

"Is this anything to do with us?"

Victor's mouth was set in a line.

"Do you need a hand with anything?" he continued.

Victor rose: "If the Church is in such a bloody hurry to help, let them get involved."

Ricky waited.

"Let them set up a dialogue with the INP, the City Government, the *Atas* – "

"The loggers," Ricky added.

Victor ignored it: "Let's have a free-for-all! Let everyone air their grievances!"

"So you're done with the Mayor. You don't want to do business with him? "

"I'm disappointed how things have turned out. That INP Lieutenant is still there. He was supposed to be removed. Now he's allocating reconciliation money, making promises about how it will be spent. First, there *isn't* any money yet! Nor is it his job -"

"And the loggers?"

"The point - which you are missing Ricky - is that this is not about loggers *per se*. It is an attempt to split people into three tribes where only one exists."

"Is that right."

"These safe havens. They've started moving towards them. Once they're in, they'll lose their land – without any of the issues being resolved!"

"And we mind because?"

"!If the Mayor had got the Church on the path of negotiated demands – even the *datus* respect the Church – it wou - "

"And you really care about the *Atas?*"

Victor twiddled a pencil: "Put it like this. What PANAMIN proposes is not the answer." Because, not that Ricky needed to know, the climax needed to be mid-August leaving one month for army sterilization of the area and a week either side. Unless people were brought back now there would not be enough confusion in the contested area for the army to bother coming! "The whole thing's a mess."

"So what?"

"The mayor is my man and he has allowed it!"

"What's the other mayor doing?"

"Paying so much a head plus food for votes at the next election."

"He was popular. 'til you unseated him."

"You've made your point -"

He looked across the desk at Ricky, suddenly wanting to hug him.

"What got into you?" Norma railed. "Look what you've done!"

"What?"

"You and your big mouth!" she stamped about. "You'll see! And it's *not* a mine!"

"If it's not a mine – "

"A rumour like that'll bring the NPA here! "

"But you'd like that."

"Yes! I shall join them!"

"Don't throw yourself away."

"And becoming a priest isn't throwing yourself away?"

"I'm trying to find my vocation."

"So am I!" She glared at him. "Either way, you've ruined – us."

"There can be no 'us'," Jack said carefully. "I belong to all people equally."

"So vain. I didn't mean that."

"Anyway, nothing's happened."

"No? A lot of people heard what you said!"

Including, he soon discovered, the Bishop. With his sermon hanging over him, Jack set off to walk the few blocks to the Western edge of town telling himself the summons could be just an invitation totally unconnected with what Norma described as his 'outburst'. No one had referred to it since. In the normal run of time it would have just been 'last week's sermon', soon forgotten.

The bustle of the Bangkerohan Market distracted him. But the sermon returned. It would have been highly marked at the seminary. As the Weather Bureau and cemetery came into sight he felt nervous. Finally there it was. Bishop's Residence. What was the Bishop like? He peered through the railings. The garden was overgrown, its lawn unswept and at the centre a large tree drooped rope-like tendrils which swayed in fringes, some having reached the ground and rooted. He turned through the gate. To either side of the path the old tree's leaves were littered. They scrunched underfoot as he approached the building. Perhaps the meeting was about his allowance?

He rang the bell. It had to be about the sermon. A rattling sound grew louder and the door opened the merest crack. "Aha!" A man with small eyes exclaimed, drawing back, leaving the door open but not inviting him in. Jack sensed him making a note of his light hair and "fish eyes" as he'd heard Western eyes called on account of their roundness. The man's scrutiny ended. "This way!" Jack stepped in, following him up a narrow corridor with polished wood floor. "In here. I am the Bishop's secretary." He cocked his head, as if expecting a reply. For a moment it occurred to Jack the man might be mad. "You will find the Bishop lucid and correct," he stated. "He may talk about using animal blood in sacrifices. Each answer is a question. We never know where he stands."

"Animal blood in sacrifices?"

"That is correct."

"You mean – tribals are allowed to incorporate ritual animal slaughter in the celebration of the Mass?"

"Very lucid."

The man withdrew leaving Jack with the upright chairs and a sense of unease he hadn't felt since a small boy waiting outside the Headmaster's Office. An eternity passed.

"Bishop Gabilon will see you now."

"I trust the matter of your stipend has been clarified?" Bishop Gabilon enquired briskly as Jack stepped into the room. "I believe you English are very fond of a cup of tea." He touched a bell. "Though of course you would not pay £40 for it."

"40 *pence* perhaps - " Jack relaxed. "But if you brew it yourself –"

"Because *if,*" Bishop Gabilon interrupted. "The workers of Indian and Sri Lankan tea plantations were paid a fair wage for a day's work, that is what it would cost."

Jack waited.

"The older you get the more people want to come to you for confession. Do you know why? Because they think you don't hear well. But I hear perfectly well. And for a long way."

He directed his attention to the inappropriateness of Jack's sermon then handed him a quote. "These are the words of Horatio de la Costa, a Jesuit. Is he alive? You don't know. Is he dead?"

Jack read the quote.

"Stop when you disagree."

"Helping the self-development of peoples – or as Christ preferred to put it, proclaiming the Good News to the poor and to captives freedom – That's not true -"

"Correct."

"- is to enter into a conflict situation. Not true either."

The Bishop nodded.

"Like the Christ we serve, we bring peace; and because we do, tyrants will have swords drawn against us -"

"Too melodramatic, don't you think?" the Bishop asked.

"In the end the people we have helped to set free may feel free to reject us. This we must accept with grace, if possible; if not, with courage."

Bishop Gabilon leaned forward.

"You see how he seeks to put himself in the centre of the conflict, centre stage? As did you. Christ taught forgiveness."

"Christ taught forgiveness -" Jack felt safe to repeat.

"But I don't recall him saying anything about equal economic development. Do you?" Jack waited. "In fact, Christ said: render unto Caesar the things that are Caesar's and to God the things that are God's. Is that right?"

"Social justice is God's."

The Bishop's expression suggested he was not used to being contradicted or argued with but was listening intently, awaiting his chance.

"I'm not saying we in the West are any better," Jack stated. "We make debtors out of poor countries by giving loans with interest they'll never escape -"

"I *see!*" Bishop Gabilon clasped his hands. "So what we are doing here is salving your Western conscience! Excuse me! I thought the congregation at the Cathedral were Filipinos!"

"The military are."

"The military is a big employer."

"And the CHDF units."

"I am re-assigning you to a small parish on the outskirts of town – an ex-rubber plantation fallen into decay – where you will have maximum opportunity to acquaint yourself with our -" Bishop Gabilon paused, "language and *customs –*"

"I merely clarified the Our Father - "

" - and to develop what is essential in any priest. Tact."

"I had to speak out about what is going on."

"Which, of course, you understand intimately."

"No."

"Did it occur to you that the people you were *lecturing* are on the outer fringes of major political disturbances? Why do you suppose the populace of Paquibato are at loggerheads?"

"Old feuds?"

The Bishop smiled. "They have been pitted against each other, *Ata* against *Ata*, *Ata* against Visayan." He glanced through the window at his secretary in conversation with a gardener on the lawn. "The principal actors, I think you will find, are PANAMIN -"

"I've never heard of it-"

" – the Mayor and, working behind the scenes but in the dominant role, *business interests*," he said, making the words sound like a man's name. "But of course you would have been too busy with your oratory to notice."

"I wasn't thinking of Paquibato."

"Such upheavals in our country are caused by the conflict of interests of highly motivated forces." They saw the secretary turn and begin heading back towards the house. "Widespread killings," the Bishop said quickly. "Can only be explained through a careful analysis of *the interplay of powerful interest groups* whose personal ambitions and business interests are served."

"You mean look at the results and you'll find the motive?"

"I mean –" the Bishop stressed softly. "God is in the heart of each man. And that is where the work is to be done. Did you think God operated in great political swathes so that when we have social justice, God arrives?"

From a window which needed cleaning, the Bishop watched Jack walk down the path towards the gate. There

195

went a brave young man. He eased a black edged Memoriam card from his breviary, looked at the picture of the recently assassinated Archbishop Oscar Romero of San Salvadore. He turned the card over, reading the words of the man whom, when he had met him at a Bishops' conference had been diffident and retiring yet had become caught up in his country's conflict. Here were the words with which Archbishop Romero had, from the pulpit, gently pleaded with ordinary soldiers in the armed forces:

> "Brothers, before an order to kill
> that a man may give, the law of God
> must prevail that says: "Thou shalt
> not kill! … In the name of God, and
> in the name of this suffering people
> whose laments rise to Heaven each day
> more tumultuous, I beg you, I implore
> you, I order you in the name of God:
> Stop the repression!"

23rd March 1980.

The next day he had been shot dead.
He tucked the card back in his breviary. The secretary was at the door. Without eye contact, the Bishop said: "Investigate very thoroughly that young priest's links in this area."

"After a short crack at the Cathedral" Jack wrote home that night. "I am being moved to an older church in an outlying area that served rubber workers before Mr. Salcedo opened

196

up the land to bananas and built the Cathedral." He paused. Norma had been so upset. "I've been asked to come back occasionally – extra Masses, help with confessions but the place sounds like a backwater." He paused again. *Just* as he was getting *involved,* to be shunted off... "I feel more like a priest now," he added. "But things aren't very clear. Politeness gets in the way of duty."

Chapter Eleven

At last, as a result of Victor's covert prompting of the Mayor, it was all happening: peace marches, rallies; people crowding back into the area hopeful of restoring situations favourable to themselves; meeting places were filling with people airing their grievances, all duly noted down by Church volunteers. The feeling was that all right-minded people welcomed the Mayor's initiative. Resolutions were made. The Church was congratulated. The list of assurances put in place by the Mayor had satisfied the majority: the remainder, confident that "pacification and reconciliation" funding would be made available to them, had settled for that.

"I congratulate you but you should have thought of this in the first place," Victor scolded the Mayor. "See how people have flooded back into the area?"

"All this will cost money -"

"Don't worry about money, my good man." He patted his shoulder. "What you're doing is well worth it and will not go unnoticed."

The Mayor tottered off.

Victor congratulated himself, leaned forward and checked his calendar. No way could they send in the army now. Later, at a date of *his* choosing, local Opposition would spot that the Mayor had earmarked funds *without due process*. He, Victor, would then suggest to Ricky that the man be disqualified. Ricky, thinking himself original, would say: "Be better to let him lose the next election." And then he, Victor, would say: "So tell the dud Mayor, if he wins the election, *none of the previous mayor's arrangements stand*. Tell him," his voice would slow, *"that I cannot be more explicit."*

He poured a large Scotch. That last bit had been easy compared with setting and lighting the fuse between the Visayan loggers and Ata *datus*: work of the highest order, very delicate. Without it, would any have welcomed the Church's peace initiative? He shook his ice cubes in the glass. *Technique!* With the mayor disqualified, none would have the authority to grant the negotiated demands; people would then genuinely riot without pattern or reason, unleashing a turmoil that would crush to pulp the fragile flower of the peace process and revitalise, magnify enmities and grievances to such proportions that the public would *beg* the government to send in the army and only the army would dare enter the area. Their actions would be swift and crude. Like a baby's bottom, the area would be wiped clean and everyone would approve. "If they can't live peaceably," they'd say. "They *belong* in reservations."

Margolas had tried to move his timing forward. Now he would see how perfect it had been. He turned. Norma was behind him. He had not heard her entering the room.

"Let me ask you one thing," Victor said. "You know Father Jack as well as anyone. Why did he say what he said that day? About the Our Father?"

"Showing off?" she shrugged.

"Well it certainly backfired," Victor said, feeling relaxed. "When is he moving?"

"Soon."

"Get your Mother to make him a food package. He'll need it out there."

Norma moved closer to her father: "What's it like, where he's going?"

"Well," Victor sat back in his chair. "It's a sleepy place. There *is* a rubber plantation, but the trees are too old.

Forty plus years. It supports a few workers, but there are various devices for keeping wages down…"

"Such as?"

"Fining men for dirty pails or for 'wounding' the trees: sometimes pay packets go missing. Usual stuff. Most of the employment is round a tobacco factory, using piece-rate leaves grown by new settlers in the interior. The rubber trees have had it."

"Who owns it?"

"No one you can rail against. An elderly Chinese who had the foresight to use his own savings."

"A Chinese?"

"Yes. Runs the local store. No doubt you'll see all that when you visit."

"It'll be very dull for Father Jack -"

Victor laughed. "They won't understand his stories about camels getting through the eyes of needles, that's for sure!"

"Is there any Church involvement?"

"Looking for a niche for yourself?" Victor scratched the back of his head. "I *think*, but you'd have to check it – church workers encouraged the factory employees to make the usual kind of demands but it didn't get them anywhere."

"How do you know?"

"It wouldn't have. The place is no different from anywhere else. Practically no machinery. Let me know what you think of it." Victor smiled.

Norma left the room.

"You have to admire the way this was seeded," Margolas sighed, flopping a marshmallow into his coffee. "The area'll go up with one tap like a bowl covered with fractures."

Marabut reached for the sugar. "What's your money on for the one tap?"

"That you won't see Victor's hand in it!" Margolas laid his spoon in the saucer.

"Unfortunately we don't have the luxury of waiting for it to play out. Biscuit?"

"Clever though. He lets the tribals get enraged about loggers entering their territory without permission from their *datus,* makes sure they know they have a *right* to be enraged by having church groups not only *tell* them but write it all down in case they forget! My money would be on him pulling the rug out from under Church."

"No. He'll pile everything on the Mayor then cream him. I particularly liked the way he called those that took bribes to shift to the safe areas 'PANAMIN *Atas'* and the principled guys, the 30 *datus* who resisted bribes 'non-PANAMIN *Atas'*! As good as being a rebel! And anti-government! Liked that."

"What's the difference between a *datu* and an *Ata,* not that it matters?"

"They're all *Ata.* The *Datus* are the leaders of the Moslem *Ata.*"

"Whatever, they're in for surprise." He picked up his phone. "It was clever because it all looked so meaningless. Still," he sighed, feeling almost kindly towards the human race, "we can't wait till Victor drops the ostrich egg. I want battle-hardened men. Crack troops. The 61st do a fast mop up. And they've been removed from the Kalingas after protests –"

"He has men. Don't attract attention."

The jangling phone woke Victor, who had been taking a nap. He sat up, his grip tightening on the receiver as he listened. This could not be! They wanted the area cleared right now and they wanted him to do it!

"Well not yourself, obviously," Margolas' voice sounded lazy. "There are a couple of battalions on standby down there. Use them."

"I don't understand -" Victor began.

"We know you don't. Do as we ask, and then we'll see."

Victor pressed his lips together. Had the date for the UN inspection been brought forward?

"I take it you feel we don't know what's going on down there?" Margolas continued icily. Victor said nothing.

"There are things, Victor, which you don't understand. Things you don't know – which you *should* know." Victor gulped. "Did you, for example – *as our man on the spot* – know that there's been a priest up there, meddling around the mine, did you know that?" Victor pursed his lips. "One of the soldiers reported it. A *Mansakan* came down trying to sell his undershorts to them."

"I – I had no idea –"

"And the mine was mentioned in the Davao City Detainee Situationer," Margolas continued. "I have a copy here –" Victor heard the sound of rustling paper. "We didn't think things went on down there that you didn't know about."

Victor pressed his lips tighter.

"Obviously you were deceived in regard to that priest -" He swallowed.

"On your own doorstep," Margolas reined in his voice to conclude the conversation. "Therefore I think, Victor, that you had better rely on our interpretation of events and timings, don't you?" He hung up.

Suddenly Victor felt fragile. Things were slipping from his hands. The area had to be cleared now and cleared fast. That's what they'd said.

"Ricky! Ricky!" he called, hurrying about the house, short of breath and frightened. "Get in here!" A couple of battalions. That would be – who should he call to deal with this? He found Ricky outside amongst the pickups.

"Are you alright?" Ricky came towards him. "Sit down."

"I need help. Fast. Get Commander Lamparas and General Ramos to Bishop Gabilon's tonight. For a meeting"

"Can you use the Bishop's house like that?"

"Unless he wants to imply he doesn't care about the Paquibato peace initiative. Deal with it. And I don't want him in the room. Or that crazed secretary."

"OK."

"Get Lamparas and Ramos to arrive separately, after me – in civvies."

Hand it to them. They'd clear the area. It was not as if he didn't have things on them. He could say - what? …impending chaos, current Mayor's 'treachery', safe havens? God help me! Let it be done!

Jack walked through the new town. It was quiet, not unlike the one the bus had stopped at on his way across Mindanao. People invited him to eat with them, their children sat on his knee, leaned on him while he ate. Patently all were short of food and apart from the "broken" rice they bought from the sole store, run by an aged Chinaman, seemed to exist on salt, *ginamos* (fish sauce) and thin vegetables grown around their houses. "If we can taste meat once a month," they said, "we are happy."

He had been back to the Cathedral twice since leaving, but a note had come from the Bishop telling him to concentrate on his new parish and discontinue the Thursday Mass. In other words, keep out of Davao.

"Why?" he had asked Norma, who had come with tinned food from Efigenia and a note expressing her genuine anguish that their Thursday lunches had become "difficult".

"Don't ask me. My father's in a poisonous mood."

Victor had sent for the sacristan.

"Have you found out which of the Fathers visited the supposed mine site?"

Reynaldo shook his head.

"It's bad enough one got up there without it being circulated around the country. Who told Father Jack about it?"

"It wasn't in the notes through the church box," the man stated simply. "I would have kept it back. The person who types the Detainee Situationers must have added it in. And told Father Jack." He knew better than to argue with Victor. "Father Jack didn't get the Detainee Situationers."

Victor exhaled.

The elderly widower was useful because he had few social contacts and never drank. Hoping the answer was 'no' Victor asked: "Did you discover how he got the tapes out to that beach office?"

"No. And you've put a stop to it -"

204

"I arranged for him to come back twice a week," Victor contradicted. "Better to *know* who's doing it than not know. It's the Bishop who's decided he's a menace. Who could that priest have been? Brother Thomas?"

"Brother Thomas keeps a clean nose."

"Keep an eye on the comings and goings."

"I will."

Victor paused. "I mean to discover his identity."

"Whose?"

"The priest who saw the supposed mine and brought back word of it!"

It was too frightening to think of. Marabut and Margolas had not laboured the point but by now the Detainee Situationer would have been read all over the country. Any NPA unit that could be spared might already be planning to open a front in Mindanao, might already be coming! God knew they were strong enough! With named battalions and commanders, in full strength like in Luzon, they sought out troubled situations, infiltrated, exploited them, encouraged the people to resist and entered into armed conflict on their behalf. Labelled 'communists', these were not rabble-rousers of the sort he had been dealing with but idealistic one time university students who had committed themselves to their cause. What a perfect platform this would be for them! An undeveloped rural area, occupied by indigenous people, and harbouring assets desired by overseas interests. The NPA had always wanted a Front in Mindanao! To stretch from one end of the Philippines to the other! It didn't bear thinking about. The mine would fail. He would lose his plantation. His family would be reduced to penury, life would be over. Because of one priest!

He strode about.

"Get a grip. Get a grip."

The area he had been asked to clear was on its way to being clear. The NPA had not arrived. If they came after the UN Inspection, he could care less! Provided he had been paid off! Oh God! Let it happen! His eye strayed to the newspapers under the chair, their upside-down headlines unnecessary over the pictures of tanks, Generals. *No one could say he had caused this.* People had choices. The safe havens were there. Where the paper was folded showed the legs of a child, presumably being carried. He winced, walked out of the room. *This was not his fault!* He'd passed on an order from Manila; a government order. Words. Which, if he hadn't, someone else would have. And the fact remained that he had sold his current crops and fulfilled the terms imposed on him within the timeframe for release from his debts. He entered his study and poured a drink. They would want to keep him sweet to keep him quiet. His hand moved towards the phone. And stopped.

Every morning when he opened his door to let in the sun, Jack could see Ah Chan across the dusty square, pottering amongst his plastic buckets, coils of rope, setting out his store. Jack would call, wave, and Ah Chan would wave back. The only two foreigners in town: he with his with his pink-white Englishness and Ah-Chan, always dressed in white singlet and black shorts, his yellowed skin and absent eyes giving him the appearance of a rock lizard, only coming alive when he turned to spit or shout a greeting.

Ah Chan always beckoned Jack over at quiet times, dragging out plastic crates for them to sit on, giving him a beer. He didn't drink himself but liked to see Jack drinking. And he liked to talk in English about his old mother, carrying cakes around their home village to sell to Malays "too lazy to make their own" - before he had come to the Philippines.

"We're exiles," Jack joked. "Were you born in Malaysia?"

Ah Chan pulled the toothpick from his mouth: "It Malaya then. I send money home. My brother family. Tomorrow no beer. No shop."

"I know. There's a Hearing about your Tobacco Factory."

"How you know?"

"I'm saying a Special Mass for the success of the Hearing. People collected money for it."

Ah Chan laughed. "They do better buy a tin of sardines!"

It was clear that people were poor. Since the decline of the rubber plantation their children had been weaned on *lugaw* (rice water gruel) instead of milk. But less clear was what was actually being confessed in Confession.

"Father, I kept dropping the tobacco bales at work," a woman murmured.

"That's not a sin."

"So I had to work downstairs," the voice went on quietly.

"For punishment."

"How is that punishment?"

"The tobacco wastes are piled by the toilet. They smell."

"You don't need to confess things like that."

"The work downstairs is heavier. The baskets of leaves weigh over 10 kilos. I carried them."

"How is that wrong?"

"I was pregnant."

"It's not good work practice -"

"I drop the bales upstairs deliberately - "

"I shouldn't worry about it... I absolve you from your sins..."

The woman rose cautiously and left Jack feeling she was somehow dissatisfied.

Gradually the subscript emerged.

"All good Catholic here Father," Ah Chan grinned one evening. "Nobody practice the birth control. They get the big family!" His grin was exceptionally inscrutable. "Or not."

"What are you saying, Ah Chan?"

"These women know how to lose the baby!"

Since Jack had left, Norma hung around the house at a loose end. Jack's comments about the mineral deposit didn't seem to have gone anywhere. He should have shut up. Now nothing was happening and she could hardly go out to the village in the valley on her own. But they had seen something. A landing strip. Or road. Whatever.

"May I ask you something?" she began brightly, approaching Victor.

"What?" he turned around, the absent look that had been haunting him barely at bay.

"Has there been any development going on over towards the mountains?"

"Did someone say there had?"

"A woman in the market mentioned a new road," she lied.

Victor nodded: "Have to take her word for it," he shrugged. Norma wandered off.

Margolas had said there were things he didn't know. Fair enough. So this was a good sign. But if things *had* started they should let him off the hook! Oh to be secure! Could anything be more sweet? To return to normal; make plans for the future! He went looking for Ricky.

"We should turn the engines over. No point mothballing the planes."

Ricky helped his father into a seat: "Well you've brightened up –".

"Just need a change of scene."

"Buckle up. Where to?"

"A general look at the area."

The plane bounced in the heat as beneath them a great void yawned up, the area which had been so swiftly cleared by military.

"Which way now?"

"Over there." Victor pointed towards the mountains. Ricky glanced down at the scars of huts in a burnt landscape. "Those loggers deserve everything they get. There's the old Tagum road. See?" he indicated a bus labouring on it. "Where now?"

"Just fly about."

From the sky old trails, overgrown at ground level could be discerned and paths, barely a foot wide, snaking on ridges between patches that natives had cleared for cultivation.

"Over that way a little," Victor pointed, seeing a break in the forest cover.

Ricky banked. "What did you say?"

"Nothing."

He had in fact sworn for below on his side lay the graded, all but surfaced road, dead ending in the beginnings of the open-face mine. Work had clearly started.

"Which way?" Ricky shouted.

"Give the engines a good work out! Keep going."

Presumably visitors would arrive by helicopter and not realise the road only went a few hundred yards. But how had they got the machinery in?

"If I keep going we'll hit the mountain!"

"Make a loop. Go home."

Sensing a change in his father's mood, Ricky pulled away, following an old track which ran like a parting through undergrowth below. He dived, enjoying the sensation of flight, the plane's shadow skimming, almost touching the trees.

The hell with it, thought Victor, anticipating lunch. He'd done his bit. The area was clear. The mine was in place. The planes were good as paid off. Their future was saved.

"Town up ahead."

"What?"

"My side." Ricky tilted the plane. Rooves, school, a market place, families crowded in the street waving up at the plane. Ricky waved back.

The journey continued in silence.

In Manila, Margolas called Marabut: "It's time to reel Victor in." But as he reached for the receiver, the phone rang. Margolas covered the mouthpiece with his hand:

"It's Victor. He wants to see us."

Chapter Twelve

Margolas glanced at the monitor. "It's him." They leaned forward to watch Victor preening in the elevator.

"Nervous?"

"No. Angry."

The elevator clanked to a halt. They heard its doors squeak open, footsteps, the knock, the door being thrust open.

"My dear Victor," Margolas forestalled him, crossing the room, arm out. "First things first. Congratulations." He nodded to Marabut who popped a champagne cork, trying to ignore Victor's body language which clearly indicated he had seen through them. He poured, handed a glass to Marabut who held it out to Victor. "We are grateful to you." But Victor wasn't looking at either of them. He had his eyes fixed on a large relief map on the wall behind Marabut.

"What, may I ask you," he demanded crossing and stabbing at the map with a finger, "is *that?*"

Margolas smiled. "How astute of you to note its significance! Our tailing pond."

"Your *what!!?*"

"Tailing pond, don't you know? The depression that takes the liquid sludge from the mine. The run-off."

"Don't worry about technicalities Victor -" Marabut urged softly.

Margolas interrupted: "Nice that you're interested. But enough to know it's clear. Like everywhere else."

"We spoke of moving scattered settlers and the *Ata* tribe -"

"We spoke of *clearing the area.*"

Margolas sipped his champagne.

"We thought you'd come to report having cleared squatters from our tailing pond. Haven't you?"

"It's an established township!"

"If you're telling us our tailing pond site is – whatever you just said – it seems you haven't done your job."

For a few moments no one spoke.

"The mine will process initially US$400,000 worth of copper ore per day as well as gold and silver by-products," Margolas said from the window.

"Put the tailing pond elsewhere!"

Margolas turned to him. "We could use Tagbarus Gulley, yes. Depending on whether the tailing line is made of wood or steel but that, according to the mine engineer, would cost an extra 60 to 80 million pesos."

"But is uninhabited?"

Margolas nodded. "One day we *may* use it. Given the life expectancy of the projected tailing pond is only 22 years - "

"It's full of people!"

"Such a humanitarian!" He stubbed out a cigarette that had been resting in an ashtray.

"Let's keep this thing in proportion Victor. How many families have you disrupted lately? Or is that these are *Visayans?*"

"You're the man on the spot," Marabut punned. "You suggest what? *Ask* the people you say are there to move? Offer compensation?"

Victor clenched his hands: "If you insist on the *cheapest* option -"

"We do."

"For quick wealth -"

"Catch fortune as she flees."

"And are determined to turn people's assets into a dump -"

"We are."

"Then *accuse them of being communist sympathizers and the army'll raid the place!*"

"The communists," Margolas said coldly, "as you well know, aren't there for them to be sympathetic to."

Suddenly Marabut jumped up. "For God's sake, man!" He smacked the map. "Create that kind of a scandal and the NPA'll be in like lightning! It'd be another siege situation like the Kalingas! How long's that been going on? Ten years? Capital leached away! Backers gone! That suit you?"

"You should have been honest with me!"

"Don't shout."

"You *lied* to me!"

"Would you have done it?"

"About Paquibato."

"So what? Took you long enough to spot."

"What will Paquibato be? Pineapples? More bananas?"

"You were happy to do it."

Victor stood, biting a finger.

"Do you want out?"

His voice came weak. He was being played like a small bird! "My *plantation,* my *planes* - "

"Is the land cleared? You phoned and said it was."

Victor moved to a chair.

"Don't bother sitting. Will you be returning to Manila when your plantation folds? I hear there are cane fields laying waste in Negros. A man *could* start again -"

Marabut placed his hand in the small of Victor's back, began steering him towards the door.

Victor pulled back.

"Finally our Victor has run out of ideas!" Margolas tutted, feeling in his jacket, producing a card and handing it to Victor. "One night's hotel credit. For old times' sake." He clapped him on the back and pushed him through the door.

Victor found himself in the corridor.

On the monitor Margolas and Marabut watched him. He stood facing the door as if he might knock. Then turned, walked head down towards the elevator.

"Properly motivated," Margolas stated. "Victor *will* achieve."

He had his back to the camera as the lift went down but the movement of an elbow suggested something being removed from a pocket. He dabbed his face. Before the elevator stopped, he pulled back his shoulders, stepped boldly into the lobby feigning purpose, crossed to Reception, pulled a card from his pocket.

Margolas picked up the phone.

"Horatio? Expect Victor Salcedo shortly. Give him all he wants. Send a special steward up. Fine, yes. And You? And Marguerite?"

Victor checked in, the hotel's glitz kicking against the helplessness suffocating him. He crossed to the window, looked out over Manila. There were the towers of Makati he remembered leaving in despair, the Hilton where he had known a false hope that had sustained him. A soft knock. He turned. In the open door stood an attractive young woman with a large basket of fruit and a floral arrangement with a card in it. She entered, placed them carefully, bobbed a submissive curtsey, stepped out backwards. Another tap. A smart young man was pushing in a linen covered brunch/drinks trolley. Victor turned his back. The young man withdrew.

As the door closed, he threw himself on the bed. *Bastards!* To clear that valley called for a military operation. The entire township needed to be surrounded, utterly destroyed. Not one Emerenciana left. And fast. But how? Because it *could* be done. But what if the settlers were themselves armed? Or barricaded themselves in while a child ran to the nearest PC or INP post? He studied the ceiling. He had his own CHDF force – but one casual word from one of them and he'd be finished. Or would it be held over him and used again and again? Blackmailed. Dispossessed. Never taste freedom again …. Bastards! *All* that Paquibato business … *Concentrate!* He pushed himself up, began to pace. Those bastards hadn't needed Paquibato at all! Just land grab! And now *this!* "To be *disassociated from the action,"* he said aloud. How had Emerenciana been cleared out with no one knowing who had done it? Some implausible story about – soldiers was it? But there had been no soldiers. Had soldiers arisen, done their work and vanished? There was a knock at the door.

"Special services Sir -" a voice called.

"Get out."

How could he be even *thinking* of it? This was not firing a few shots into someone's thatch. This was *murder.* The *theory* was a challenge, yes, but the *commission?* And they knew he'd do it, Margolas and Marabut. He gripped his face in his hands. They were waiting for him to figure out how to do it, to guess! Because there was a way. Oh yes *they'd* been in on clearing out Emerenciana for their mine road! They wouldn't tell him how they'd done it or he'd hold it over them. And *their* hands must be kept clean so it had to be *him!* He knelt by the bed. "Dear God! You must understand," he glanced up at the ceiling. "I'm in too deep -" He got to his feet, began to pace. To finish and be done. But how? Who and how?

Jack had not seen anything of the Salcedos in a good while but had been distracted by rumblings in his own sleepy town. 'Mr. Chan is too clever,' people told him. Several months before he had come, in an attempt to resist change, Mr. Chan had transferred his more docile workers to a new factory shed, leaving the 'trouble makers' who'd wanted change on a lower wage at the old place. Gradually that group had been told there was a shortage of tobacco leaves and had been laid off. The situation had rumbled on for a long time before the disenfranchised workers had turned to an out-of-town Social Action Group, who had taken Ah Chan and his tobacco works to court. Nothing had come of the initiative and peace had returned to the township, because 'that was the way it was' and everyone accepted that.

Norma, however, who visited Jack on and off with food parcels because her parents encouraged it, had said they should *not* accept it and had offered to make a phone call to kick-start proceedings. For her part, the issue validated her constant appearances in the village and prevented loose tongues ascribing baser motives to Jack for allowing her to spend time with him. "I very much doubt anyone even read their Complaint," she'd shrugged.

"It'd be good if you could do something but - "

"I know. Keep you out of it."

"Did that woman from New Cebu ever turn up at the beach or market place?"

"No. Can't you travel? We could go! Do you just have to stay out of Davao City?"

"Right now wouldn't be right - "

Since that time, Jack had not seen Norma but assumed she had been busy because Judgment had been given against Mr. Chan. He'd been ordered to reinstate workers he'd laid off for picketing, pay everyone the same wage, provide sick leave, maternity leave, hospitalization benefits, Christmas bonuses, establish a Grievance Committee to hear complaints... provide separation pay for those wishing to leave... all of which sounded unlikely to Jack as he glanced across at Ah Chan putting out his plastic buckets, his pails, his coils of rope and wire, giving them a quick flick with a feather duster before sitting on his stool, leaning forward on one arm to read his paper in the sun and pick his teeth with a match. The phrase "Miss Norma is very clever," was around every dusty corner and the individual households, poor as they were, could be said to be celebrating.

This court 'victory' could not end well, Jack realised, because Ah Chan knew exactly what was going on in Philippine society and understood Man's nature. And he clearly felt no malice towards the people who thought they had achieved some kind of victory over him. His manner had not changed, nor had he varied his daily routine.

Though Jack felt detached from the issue, there had been two occasions when the Social Action Group – students from Davao City who visited the small townships - had run a surgery in a small shed and caused him to wonder should he, as a priest, have discouraged them from building the hopes of these people, happy in their ragged *barrio,* slapping each other's shoulders, going home to their rice and *ginamos;* happy even to spend their day's wage on stale cakes from Ah Chan's store for "the priest to eat" …? He had never known any of them dislike or be critical of Ah Chan: if anything they understood Ah Chan's position. Was he being patronizing to them? Cynical about Ah Chan? Or was this mental separation he was experiencing exactly what the Bishop had intended? Was Norma's involvement – because that was probably what had been keeping her away, - doing 'his' people any favours?

Norma, however, was unaware of those outcomes. Having made one phone call to the Clerk of the Court to prevent the case languishing indefinitely, as usually happened with peasant complaints, she had not given another thought to the tobacco workers nor made a follow-up call. Local injustice would always be there and was not her job. Her job was to repair the breach Fr. Jack's relocation had caused in the Detainee Situationer chain and after much searching and many dead ends, she had discovered how to get Notes from the Cathedral to the beach office. The Detainee Situationer would not be sabotaged! Word of exactly who was doing what to whom, why and how in Davao City and its surrounds would be known again – nationally and internationally! All these major injustices, at the root of them greed over land! That was real! A fight worth dying for!

Her car had scrunched to a halt outside The Lodge.

"God guide me," Brother Tomas whispered, clenching moist hands in his pockets. He opened the door before she could ring.

"I was passing," Norma said fixedly. "Father Jack has left the Cathedral."

218

"Indeed."

"No doubt everything will carry on as usual -" Her eyes had narrowed in emphasis.

Brother Tomas' head moved as if to convey difficulty verging on the impossible.

"I have resumed the 10 o'clock Mass -" he said weakly, the strain of listening for nuances in her voice making him sweat.

"Well I wish you well," she smiled. "By the way – a new altar boy is starting on Thursday. He's never served Mass before -" She waited, seeking any slight movement in Brother Tomas' face. "Quite an undertaking for a small child -" She waited. "Don't you agree?"

"Serving Mass *is,* as you say, an undertaking," Brother Tomas repeated. "Especially for a small child."

Their eyes met.

"Well, I hope you will keep an eye on him."

"My duty, as a priest, is to see Mass is served properly." His eyes were quite cold. "If any training is necessary, I shall arrange it."

Norma departed.

Victor looked in the mirror, puffing out his chest, taking strength from the fact he was staying at the Manila Hotel. God should understand he'd wanted to do things humanely. Now he just wanted to *do* them. He coughed. Picked up the phone. "Operator! Get me -" What was he doing calling General Thon, the man whom even Marcos feared? He was calling the one person whose bread and butter was terror, whose information network was accurate! He waited, sweating.

"Victor," a cold voice answered.

"General, is that you?"

"Remember. I am a phone call away."

Victor shuddered.

"I am from Min- "

"I know who you are."

"Some months ago, a woman came to me for protection." Victor tried to keep the strain from his voice. "She alleged - "

To his amazement the General interrupted: "I know about the work you are doing. President Marcos thinks highly of you."

Afraid of being switched off, yet not wishing to contradict, Victor pressed on. "But my reasons now -"

"Quite," the General cut him off. "There were no soldiers in the area. But if there is anything," he stressed the 'any', "I can do to help, at *any* time..." He gave his special number. And hung up. Click.

Victor flopped on the bed. He had spoken to General Thon; the man who dealt in terror, the torturer. And had been unable to phrase what he wanted to say. But wait! The General had been prepared to speak to him. His call was clearly not unexpected. He was on the right track. The questions he'd wanted to put held less significance. There had been soldiers. They'd been violent. Irregularities had occurred. He lay on his back, shut his eyes, pushed his fingers in his ears. The Lost Command! Was that it? That shadowy force supposedly made up of ex-soldiers, who lived cut off from society, whose trademark was necklaces of human ears strung across tracks they didn't want explored. They came. They killed. They vanished without trace. He had never believed in them. Some said they didn't exist but that General Thon used tales of them to instill fear and achieve his

220

objectives… Others that they were under orders from him. He picked up the phone once more.

Efigenia reached for a glass of water. She could not sleep. The clammy night hung at the window: the house made sounds. Soon morning would come and she would wait for evening. Then night, and she would wait for day.

As day broke, Jack heard grumbling through the walls of his neighbours' house. He tried to sleep. Where previously they had been congratulating each other on having made a stand for Justice, now they were cowed and beaten. At each other's throats. Because they'd learned that the tobacco shed or 'new factory' as the Court papers had it, was not owned by Ah Chan but by his daughter-in-law so he had no assets. And further he'd declared himself bankrupt, wound up his business so nothing could come of their efforts except that the remote possibility of being reinstated had been taken from them. Crying came from the neighbours' house, great wails of blame rising, shouts of having listened to friends…. By day, those who'd gone to the new shed hung onto their jobs, refusing to come out in defence of those who'd stayed behind and protested on everyone's behalf … People passed each other with sour looks. And Jack prayed: "What is my role in this as a priest?" No answer came. Head down, he set off across the Square. Seeing the Catholic Father walking towards him, Ah Chan withdrew to the back of the store feeling uncomfortable. *He* knew he still owned the factory. The priest would have figured he still owned the factory. The people would soon realise he still owned the factory. He pulled off a worn flip flop, turned it over, picked at the base.

Jack walked straight into the store, took down a beer, tapped it on the counter: Tap! Tap! Tap! Tap! Ah Chan shuffled forward, eyes down, pushed the bottle opener at him – glancing sideways at the little shrine to his ancestors, the Chans of the world, blinking in the dark. Wrestling with the top, Jack suddenly knew with a swell of joy, what he was supposed to do. His questions about the nature of Faith, Norma's about its application – the church workers busyness with *rights* – these were important, yes, but his work was forgiveness, love, repair, new hope. He took a swig of the beer, looked gently at Ah Chan hunched behind the counter expecting a scolding and gave him a wide smile. Slowly a smile spread on the Chinaman's face.

Victor wiped his mouth with the back of his hand, wiped his hand on his trousers. There was nowhere on the plane to wash. At the airport he'd swilled water round his mouth, wetted his fingers, ground them into his ears. He'd wanted to sink in a river, wash his armpits, put his head under water, leave his filthy clothes – come out clean!

The second time he'd called General Thon, a different voice had answered.

"General Thon is on an overseas trip. He is not in Manila."

"But I've just spoken to him! This is important!"

"He is not here."

The receiver had been replaced. Victor had had the call put through again.

"This is Victor Salcedo from Mindanao. I must speak to someone who – can – advise me."

There was a pause as if a hand were over the receiver.

"A car will come to take you to the airport." Click.

What did it mean? He packed hurriedly. The speaker had not asked where he was staying? How could a car come? He went downstairs, stepped out of the hotel and waited. No sign of a taxi or airport limousine. He felt stupid looking about. A tout sidled up.

"Airport?"

"Go away."

"Mr. *Salcedo?*" He gave a greasy smile, offered his hand. Victor recoiled, but followed him to a dirty Chevrolet with dented sides. "Get in." The man inclined his head politely.

After a drive in which Victor's lungs filled with the man's smell, he pulled into a lay-by, turned to face Victor, opening his fingers like scissors and placing them on either side of the ear closest Victor, he grinned, looked him in the eye. "I take it you can hear me?"

He had the look of a man who might once have been military but was now overweight, carnal, slimy and gave off an aura of delighting in degradation, filth. He pulled a map from the door pocket, spread it on his knee, turned to Victor – pushing it across. His flies were undone. As he talked, his stubby finger slid up roads, down tracks towards the settlement of New Cebu, circling, dredging its obscene way across the houses – all carefully drawn in – speaking of the women and children there, beginning to pant. The map suddenly rose on his knee; his right hand slid under it as without shame, he brought himself to climax, while he talked, his breath interrupted, his voice rising, using the intimacy to make Victor, by remaining silent, a party to it. When it was over he slammed the map shut with sticky fingers, looked Victor in the eye: "And no witnesses. Suit you?" Victor stared ahead. The man wiped his hands on his shirt front. "The bodies will go in the lake." Victor said nothing. "And because we don't exist, no one will come looking – " He looked at Victor, shrugged. Started the engine.

As they drove, he whistled. Reaching the airport turnoff, he unstuck a damp envelope from inside his singlet, handed it to Victor. "Phone number and password. My men are encamped within target reach now. Waiting for your instruction. Or that of the default party if you bottle out." He stopped a good walk from the airport building, began picking his nose. "I don't go any farther." Victor hurriedly opened the door, got out, stuffing the clammy envelope in his pocket. "C'mere," the man said, forcing Victor to lower his face towards him. "The clocks running."

At home, in the darkness of his horse's stall, Victor let out his anger. "How *dare* they?" he asked his horse. Barbary backed away from him. He kicked the stall. The bank manager, his *own* bank manager, had seen an opportunity and offered him. He'd been *sold, yes sold* to the directors of PANAMIN by his own bank manager! Why hadn't he seen that Paquibato was too far from the mine site to be significant... except as a depot town...? The horse's large frightened eyes blinked at him. For the price of two planes and a banana crop they'd got all that fertile land and the timber on it! And he, Victor Salcedo, would carry the moral guilt for the disenfranchised people, the mayhem that was erupting, *when all along* the only thing they'd set out to do was clear the tailing pond!

Why hadn't it occurred to him? They'd get their tailing pond whether he responded or not: they'd set a time limit on his option to make that phone call. Yes, but they'd got the *Paquibato area too!* They hadn't needed him at all! Without him they'd clear New Cebu away like they'd cleared Emerenciana. **But they wouldn't have got the Paquibato area...** He'd been made a fool of! The horse shifted nervously. Noting it, the stable cat climbed down and sat between her and Victor, now too angry to go into his own house or speak. He was a means to another man's dishonest goals. That hurt his pride and brought his social standing, his manhood into question.

Ricky saw him walking back to the house, caught up with him: "Have a good trip?"

Victor ignored him.

"What's eating you?"

"I have worries."

"So get Commander Lamparas or General Ramos up and ask them how -"

"You think I can have men like that in the house at a time like this?"

"A time like what?"

"I am up to *here!*" He brought his hand up to his chin.

"You found a buyer for the crop; you renegotiated the loan -"

Victor continued glaring.

"I see."

"You see *nothing!* I can't be seen with members of the military when we have a situation of unrest on our doorstep."

"Because it'll look as if we had some interest in the outcome of the Paquibato situation?"

"Which we do not."

He wiped his face. Now was not the time to unburden.

"Is it land? You said there's always land -"

"I think we can come out of it Ricky. Never use land as security. Don't buy what you can't afford." He limped ahead into the house.

In unobtrusive dress and head scarf, Norma settled in at the back of the Cathedral, rosary beads in hand, head dipped as the daily Mass goers passed her on their way to their pews. In the sacristy, Brother Tomas sweated. Miss Salcedo had said Thursday. The accumulated messages were in a sealed envelope in the tabernacle, the Sacristan doubtless knowing they had not been passed on. He felt sick to the stomach. Suppose this went wrong? The only boy on the Server's rota was Leon, a 14-year old heavily into football and unlikely to have any connection with the channels that needed to be kept open.

"Father?" he turned. It was the Sacristan. "Leon has a fever. Shall I serve?"

Surely not the Sacristan!

"If nobody turns up, that would be appreciated."

"Were you expecting someone?"

"Leon may have asked a friend."

The Sacristan smiled. Being a person without power himself, he delighted in putting weaker persons on the spot. And Brother Tomas' incapacity to lie rendered him weak.

"Someone *is* here!" announced the Sacristan, turning.

Brother Tomas spun to see him tousling the hair of an eight - year old boy, scrubbed clean, clutching a school bag. *It could not be him.*

On the altar the child had to be told to fetch this, return that, put that over there, bring it back. But there was an intensity in his eyes…. The Offertory came. His back to the people Brother Tomas unlocked the tabernacle, lifted out the cloth covered chalice, the envelope balanced between the flat board on top of the chalice and the cloth covering it. He returned to the altar, placed the chalice before him and genuflected.

From the back of the Cathedral Norma, hands clenched, watched his lips move as if this Mass were no different from any other. She saw him uncover the chalice, laying the cloth and board aside, lift out, raise the Host, genuflect, the congregation's heads bowed before him.

"Let this be the right child," he prayed. "And protect him."

"Lord, I am not worthy…"

He descended to the altar rail and distributed communion: returned and sat in the chair to one side of the altar, head bowed in thanksgiving, not looking up while the new boy cleared the altar.

Thanksgiving over, he rose, returned to the altar, genuflected, folded the cloth, slid aside the board under which he had left the envelope. *It had gone*! Sitting at one side, the picture of innocence, the boy continued praying.

Heart still thumping, Brother Tomas replaced the board and cloth on the chalice, genuflected, returned them to the tabernacle, locked it, pocketed the key and turned to face the congregation.

Norma left the church. Had he got it? He was so short she had seen nothing but his arms reaching across the altar, pulling things towards him. But she watched him skip down the Cathedral steps clutching his satchel, like any other boy, glad to have had the morning off school to serve Mass. The papaya seller too watched. No one had ever asked him to serve Mass. He'd like to have gone to school and had shoes and ended up with a job mending automobiles. He wiped the cloth over his glass case. This was the best he could hope for from life: better than work as a tout.

The eight-year old ran on. He behaved normally at school. After school he handed the envelope to his sister who kissed him and gave him a peso. She phoned Norma.

"He'll never never tell! He feels brave!"

"Don't give him any information."

"I'll take it to college tomorrow and pass it – "

"Sssh."

She sped along the beach road. Job done! Detainee Situationer on track! Her involvement with it over! And Jack's! New space opening up. To do – what? She upped the volume on the radio. To get Emerenciana and the children together! Jack's idea that she should wait was unrealistic and unfair. He lacked drive. She roared up the drive to Mansion Salcedo and entered the house whistling, a sound she knew infuriated her parents.

Her father came out to block her way.

"What?"

"I want you to stay away from the area towards the mountains."

"Why?"

"Because I say so."

"Hah!" Norma brushed past him.

"Come back here!"

"Who said I wanted to *go* there?"

"Norma -" he placed a hand on her shoulder.

"Leave me alone!"

He pulled his hand back.

"You are my daughter. I - worry about you -"

"Don't."

"There are things you don't know -"

"*I know what I know!*"

"But - *I know.*"

"What?"

He lowered his voice. "People are watching you - "

"I know *that!*"

"It is you who types the Detainee Situationers…"

"It is not!"

Her indignation surprised him.

"Stop now."

"I do *not* type up the Detainee Situationers!" she shouted. "This is *my* life!"

"Then care for it! You knew you were followed! So who put a tail on you?"

Norma shrugged.

"Me!"

"How *could* you!"

"To protect you."

"From what?"

"You pass 'gossip' to the NPA -"

"I've never met an NPA in my life! I wish I had!"

"You meddle and - draw attention to yourself - " he fumbled.

"So there *is* going to be a mine? Is that why Father Jack was sent away? For mentioning it?"

"Do as I say!" Victor shouted: "Stay in Davao!"

"And not visit Father Jack?"

"Visit him, yes."

Norma shook her head. "Even if there were a mine, which I don't believe there is, it's nothing to do with you!"

"*Which is why I can't protect you. If* there is any truth in it!"

"There isn't a mine!"

Victor stood: "Let Fr Jack stand for social justice if he wants! He's a priest! It's a vocation!"

"And armed struggle isn't?"

Chapter Thirteen

As the night drew on, Victor did not come to bed. Efigenia tapped on Ricky's door.

"Would you go in and see what your father is doing?" Ricky reached for his dressing gown. Efigenia went down to the kitchen. There was something ungodly about being out of bed and alone at this time of night. She opened and closed the fridge door, tightened the taps, wandered about. After a while Ricky reappeared.

"He's on the floor -"

"On the *floor*?"

"In his study. Looking at photographs."

"This is very odd."

"His desk's covered with bits of paper – "

"Is this to do with the plantation?"

"The numbers weren't big enough. No dollar or peso signs. Saw the word Tagum."

"Did you speak to him?"

"I said can I help you in any way?"

"And?"

"He said, 'the road to Hell – is paved with good intentions'."

When Efigenia opened the room door, Victor was seated at his desk talking to himself. He balled up a piece of paper and threw it towards the bin.

"Victor," she said sharply from the door. "What are you doing?"

"I have phone calls to make."

She crossed to him: "What are these photos doing on the floor?"

"That's my mother. She was a very good woman."

"Yes. I remember. She was."

"She raised us right, me, my brothers and sisters. Wouldn't you say?"

"Well certainly she did, yes."

He dropped to the photo.

"Will you please come to bed soon?"

"What is 'soon' – " Victor repeated after her. "You go to bed Efigenia. Soon will come soon enough."

Later in the night he joined her. They lay in bed together, not sleeping, not understanding each other.

Morning came. Efigenia pinged the blind up: "Come, Victor! A new day! Let's be happy!"

He looked at her girlish, childish glee. She came and sat on the bed next to him.

"Sleepyhead! All this going to Manila! Too much stress!" She stroked his head.

"I try."

"And you do very well. We depend on you. So let's get up, have a shower and shave, put on a clean shirt and *be cheerful!"*

Victor smiled wearily.

"We don't want you suffering from nervous exhaustion or whatever it's called these days -"

Victor got up and dressed. He went downstairs. The children, as usual, were milling about the breakfast table. He felt overwhelmed with love for them. The way the light glinted off their hair, the purity of their skins seemed beautiful to him. Their eyes, when they smiled, lit up his life in a unique way. Even when they squabbled, they were beautiful.

He sat down, aware of the sunbeams flickering off the cut glass of the orange juice pitcher, the reflection of the colours beyond the window on the silver cutlery.

"Will you have tea or coffee this morning Mr. Salcedo?" Loretta was asking.

"Well done Loretta," Efigenia encouraged. "See, she's giving you a choice!"

"Should I have the vehicles serviced today?" Fredo asked. "I'm taking a run out past the piggery so – and I could check on the experimental bananas -"

"You'd better, yes," Ricky chipped in.

"That'll show those Americans," Efigenia nodded, buttering Victor's toast. "Thinking they can throw the Salcedos!"

"Once a Salcedo, always a Salcedo!" Guinaldo shouted.

The adults laughed.

"Where's Norma?"

"She had something to tell Fr. Jack."

"Did she say so Fredo?"

"I caught her leaving."

"Hurry up children! The driver's waiting!"

The children drifted off in their school uniforms.

"We were lucky to get them into that school," Efigenia said approvingly. "It's a very good school,"

Victor smiled at his cutlery.

"You have done well and you need congratulating," Efigenia continued. "It isn't said often enough."

He smiled tiredly. The compliment didn't lift him as it might once have done.

"Why don't we have another family picnic on the beach when the children get back from school?" Efigenia asked. "Let's have some 'together' time!"

Was he even listening?

"Pardon? Of course. Yes." He looked at his watch, began to eat his egg vigorously.

After the picnic Victor dozed on the beach but as the sun withdrew and shadows lengthened, the sea grew dark and the sand grey, Efigenia felt him tensing up. He checked and rechecked his watch, suddenly stood and hastened towards the house.

"Victor?" Efigenia hurried after him. "Are you alright?"

"I have things to do."

They reached the house. He ignored her.

"Victor?"

"What?"

Her eyes swept round: "Norma's not back. Did you and she fall out? I - I heard you both arguing yesterday –"

"I gave her permission to visit Fr Jack," Victor snapped. "Why would she hurry back?"

Efigenia shrugged. Norma did overnight there when she was mad at him.

"Don't let her upset – " she began, but his door had slammed.

With the children in bed and the maids gone for the weekend, a heaviness, settled on the house. The sound of Victor lifting and replacing, lifting and replacing the receiver came to her – but no speech. Finally he appeared in the doorway.

"I need to speak to you."

She followed him into his study.

"The position – " Efigenia waited. "In a nutshell – unless I clear some land for a third party – we lose our plantation."

Her mouth fell open.

"Do you understand what I'm saying?"

"Don't be ridiculous!"

"It is not ridiculous. It's happening."

"Who has done this to us?"

"A government department offered to pay off our debts on the planes and various loans -"

"Then we're alright!"

"If I do something for them."

"*Do* it."

Victor bit at his thumb.

"What do they want you to do?" Efigenia pursued. "No. Don't tell me what you have to do! *Let me tell you what I expect!* I expect you to protect your family! To put your family first."

"You don't know what they're asking."

"*Can* it be done?"

"It can be *done* -"

"Then *do* it!"

"This is – land clearance. On a massive human scale –"

"Are you a man or a mouse?"

"I'm not talking about parking outside one or two homesteads and frightening people into moving! This is an entire township! Look!" Victor snatched photos from the floor. "Look at our children. There will be children! Grandparents!"

"*Put your own family first!*"

"Can you ask me to kill women and children and old people?"

"I'll ask the man of the family. Where is Ricky?"

"Keep him out of this. I'm not having a child of mine burn in Hell for eternity!"

"In *Hell*?"

"So you believe in your Shrine's Infant of Prague and not in Hell?"

"!It's not as if you haven't caused death before -"

"You think that?"

"I surmise."

"A *township* with *roads* and *houses* and *fields* and *orchards* – "

"*And this is a plantation with roads and houses and people and* - Who wants it?"

"A mining company -"

"So Father Jack was right!"

"They want to use that valley as a tailing pond for sludge."

"Then let them have it!" Efigenia said fiercely. "This is *nothing* to do with us! Our duty before God is to protect our children!"

"You want me to kill upwards of 500 people?"

"You're *weak*!"

" - people like yourself, throats slashed, bodies thrown in a lake - "

"A big company wants the land! Give it to them!"

"- children like ours, running from buildings, shot, pinned down by roughians, raped - "

"They won't have title to the land! They shouldn't be there!"

"I won't do it."

Efigenia regrouped.

"Is this Father Jack's sermon about the *Our Father?*" she said gently.

"No. I'm not comfortable with murder."

"But someone's offered to help you?"

"Yes."

"So you don't have to do it yourself -"

"In a sense – no. But if I give the word, it goes ahead."

"!I think you'll find whether you commission it or not, it will go ahead – (!)"

"True. But if it goes ahead without me, our debts are not paid."

"And the plantation folds."

Victor nodded.

"So you are making a fuss about nothing. You should be thankful they're so desperate to have a name attached to the project that you're being rescued."

"They are covering their tracks, in case something comes out."

"Which it doesn't. In this country."

For a moment they were quiet. She put her hands on his shoulders, began gently massaging his neck. His head fell forward. She saw tears drip on his desk. Her mouth tightened. "I'm sure all this can be resolved," she said calmly. "You've always been wonderful." She rested her hands on his shoulders: "Let's have an early night. It's Saturday tomorrow. See if you don't feel better –"

He pulled away, turned to face her: "I have to give the word before dusk *tonight.* I should have made my mind up last night but – it's set to go -"

Efigenia's eyes skidded across his desk and settled on a piece of paper.

"You have to make a phone call?"

Victor nodded: "I can't." His head dropped.

"Well I *can!*" Efigenia snatched up the piece of paper.

"Give that back!"

"You unburdened yourself on *me* so that *I* would do it for you! Coward!"

Victor stood: "Give me that paper!"

"You're not fit!"

She stalked from the room. He ran round the desk, pursued her downstairs as the parlour door slammed shut and the key turned.

"Open this door!"

Behind him, light was draining from the sky. In a few seconds dusk would give way to dark. He heard her pick up the phone, dial. He banged on the door. She was speaking:

"Who is this"

"The person you would expect," said a deep voice. "Password?" On the bottom of the paper a word was written. Efigenia pronounced it.

"Putting you through."

"You want to go ahead?" asked a military voice. "You give your word?"

"I do. Go ahead," Efigenia repeated in as firm and deep a voice as she could muster. The phone clicked dead. She opened the door onto Victor, standing in the darkening hall, balled up the note, dropped it at his feet and walked past him up the stairs. Victor followed her.

"Happy now? Men are getting into vehicles, their hands turning ignition keys. They are driving up roads quietly. Under their seats are weapons: *parangs*, rifles, shot guns -"

"Shut up."

"When they get within a certain distance of their quarry, they will stop, abandon their vehicles slightly off road and fall into formation." His voice began to get louder. "Because this will be a military operation. Make no mistake. These disgraced men were once soldiers. They have nothing to live for, nothing to fear. Society is done with them. They have less status than prisoners. All they can look forward to is outings such as this when their animal wants are satisfied. Their sexual gratification -"

238

Efigenia blocked the stairway: "I'm not listening to this -"

But Victor followed her, pushing in the bedroom door, his voice getting louder: "Many of them perverted, will enjoy full play on tiny children pulled from their beds! But first they must creep up on the houses. They have military photographs showing the town layout, the routes and tracks. Nothing will happen until the signal to begin when the place is surrounded. At that moment, all will move forward together."

"The dogs will bark! They won't make it!"

"Poisoned meat is thrown to the dogs as is done here in common burglaries," Victor stated.

"You should be saying thank you to me! I saved us!"

"You didn't have to - "

"We have to *live* - "

"We would have survived -"

"On Norma's beach?" She threw herself on a chair.

"At this moment," Victor looked at his watch. "They will be very near the township. The people will have said their prayers and climbed into bed. The little ones will already be asleep. They will have plans for the next day, fish they are drying, crops half harvested -"

"What you are saying -" Efigenia said slowly. "Doesn't seem real to me. Where are you going?" She followed him to the door. "I suppose you won't forgive me now. I *saved* you."

"Not for me to forgive you -"

"Such a saint!"

"I know exactly what I am."

"Where are you going?"

"To be alone."

239

"Don't leave me here – "

"So pray. What's the matter? Can you hear the children screaming, see fathers dragging daughters out from under savages?"

"Shut up!"

The sun had barely slid through the blinds when there was a knocking at their front door.   Efigenia sat up, listened. Ricky got it.

"For Mr. Salcedo."

She heard the courier's bike receding. She got dressed.

"What was it?" she asked, coming downstairs. "You opened it?"

"It's the documents letting us off the interest on the planes - "

"Anything else?"

He turned them over. "Debt clearance documents from the bank. You want to see them?"

"Heavens no!"

She returned upstairs, dressed, attended to her face and hair, selected a smart blouse and shoes and surveyed herself in the mirror. The first day of the rest of her life. She went downstairs, settled the younger children round the table.

"Find your father and tell him breakfast is ready."

Entering the breakfast room looking dishevelled, Victor found her sitting at the head of the table. Dragging his eyes and feet, he slunk to the side, sat in her chair. She was eating unnecessarily fast. From the other end of the table, Ricky looked worriedly at his father, pushing his food aimlessly about the plate and his mother, leaning over in front of a child, cutting Victor's food loudly into small pieces, her cutlery scourging his plate.

Victor barely noticed. The bodies wouldn't sink. Someone would find one. Or two. Or some relative would turn up…. Men like that wouldn't do a body count. Perhaps that was the point of necklaces of ears across tracks. Keep the area closed. Until the valley filled with mine sludge… Looking up he found himself alone at the table.

He didn't know what to do. The house around him was coming to life but he couldn't get started. Someone laughed. He narrowly passed Efigenia in the corridor:

"I've asked Ricky to manage things 'til you feel more like yourself. Desk key?" She held out her hand. "Snap out of it Victor."

"I need to see a priest."

"Planning to cause us more trouble? I warn you -"

"I'm finished Efigenia. I'm frightened."

"You're unstable."

"Get Father Jack." He looked at her. "I won't mention – 'things'."

"Don't."

"I promise."

"Ricky can fetch him for lunch. And Norma. But he can't stay the night. He'll have Mass tomorrow -"
She trotted off.

Ricky cruised into Fr. Jack's township, heat bouncing off his car. What a dump! Lathe and plaster houses sweating in the sun: a dog drawing a foot across it's chest like a violin bow, taking a sharp nip at its flank, yelping. A man in shorts and singlet looking up. Yellow, dusty place! He parked. Already people were assembling to see who had come.

He rapped on Jack's door.

241

"Ricky!"

"I've come to get you for lunch."

"Am I allowed? The Bishop –"

"Father says."

"I'll lock up. Excuse me."

"Where's Norma?"

"She left."

"This heat is intolerable!"

"Stand inside," Jack called, reappearing and padlocking his front door.

"Where are you going Father? Who is that?" The villagers' questions followed them to the car. "When are you coming back?"

Ricky shook his head: "That would drive me wild!"

Jack opened a window.

"Close that. The car has air-con."

"Sorry. Forgot."

"Remember us driving around the plantation a few months ago?" Ricky grinned, turning towards him.

"A few months? It seems longer -"

"You were new."

"Are your parents OK?"

Ricky changed his grip on the wheel: "My father's been under a lot of pressure. Where did you say Norma was?"

"I didn't."

"You know but won't say!"

"You think that?" Jack laughed.

"*I* think you think it's up to her to tell us, not you! Or she's up to something so you're not saying."

"How about we fell out and she took off?"

"Did you?"

"No! But as you say, it's not my business."

Ricky flicked on the radio.

"Here we are!" Mansion Salcedo looked grander than Jack remembered. "C'mon in -" It was quiet. "Do you want to wash up?" And cool. The guest wash room was unchanged: cardinal red tiles on the floor, a new piece of lemon shaped soap, folded napkin … He was hunting for a bucket to swill the WC when he remembered *it flushed!* He stepped into the hallway. Stopped. The dynamic of the house had changed. There was a faint food smell but no sound.

"Jack? Fr Jack? We're in here!" Efigenia called from the lounge. Why hadn't she come to greet him? And where were the children? The maids? He stood in the lounge doorway; saw Victor staring at him from the sofa, Efigenia standing by the window. Ricky had not come in.

"How are you both?"

Victor's eyes got large. "Where's Norma?"

"Is she not back yet?"

"Where is Norma?"

"She stayed Thursday night - "

"And then?"

"It's not for me to say."

Victor stood: "Are you refusing to tell me where my daughter is?" He crossed to Jack. "She believed the NPA were in the area."

"Did she?"

Efigenia turned on Jack. "Because of your sermon!"

"I told her they weren't – " Victor said, wide-eyed. "She didn't believe me - "

"You!" Efigenia shouted at Victor. "This is your fault! She's gone looking for them!"

"Steady on!" Jack got between them. "Norma stayed Thursday night. After lunch on Friday she took off. I can give you my word she did not go looking for the NPA."

"Thank God!" Efigenia dropped on a chair. "I'm sorry for my outburst. I worry."

"You can ask her all about it yourselves later today. She may choose not to tell you but it's not my place -"

"She is her own person" Efigenia rose. "Let me get you a drink. We are forgetting our manners."
She left the room. Jack sat down.

Victor remained staring at Jack. Suddenly he crossed, hesitated, reached for the arm of Jack's chair as if about to kneel. At that moment Efigenia appeared in the doorway with the pitcher.

"What are you doing Victor! Don't embarrass Father!"
Victor struggled to his feet, returned to his place, eyes down. Efigenia was her old self, chattering, flattering. Victor's eyes stayed down. Suddenly he spoke.

"So where did she go, if she wasn't looking for the NPA?"

"Ttt Victor! Norma has *many* friends!" Efigenia scolded.

"She had intended to go straight home from my place but swung by the beach – "

"You *see!*"

"- and phoned me from the office – the church have an office there - to give me some good news and say she was giving someone a ride home. And might stay the night."

"Very sensible, you see? So let us have lunch!" Efigenia encouraged the men to rise.
Victor remained seated. "Stay the night where?"

"I've told you more than I should – " Jack turned to him. "Because you were worried."

"Stop pestering Father – "

"Towards Tagum?" Victor's voice shook.

"She'll tell you when you see her."

Efigenia moved towards Jack, colour leaving her face, fingers clawing her skirt, her breath distorted. Jack felt uncomfortable. Victor closed in.

"A valley? With a lake?"

Jack said nothing.

"For the love of God – " Victor shouted. "Was it New Cebu?"

Jack looked from one of them to the other.

Efigenia began to scream, her screams ringing off the glassware, hitting the windows. Neither man moved. With difficulty they heard loud banging on the front door.

"They've found her!" Efigenia shrieked, rushing at Jack, hammering his chest with her fists. Victor pulled her off, held her. "*You!* Because of *you!*" her rasping breath louder than the hammering. They heard the front door open and excited speech. Ricky appeared in the doorway, addressed his mother:

"There's a woman at the door. She wants to see you." His eyes took in the scene.

"Tell her to go away!" Efigenia shrieked.

"I'll come – " Victor forced Efigenia into a chair.

"There are children with her -"

"Get rid of her!"

Suddenly Efigenia leapt from her chair and ran past Victor and Ricky to the front door. Beyond it in bright sun stood Emerenciana, smiling, and a few paces back of her, two youngsters holding the hands of a toddler.

"Get out!" Efigenia shrieked, flinging out her arms. "Get away! Leave me!"

245

"You have your miracle Señora. The Infant of Prague -"

"Go to Hell!"

Emerenciana was shocked. "But I came to say Thank You Señora. Your Shrine. Now you can have Masses -"

Efigenia slammed the door.

Slowly she crept to the main room, dropped into a chair. Victor came, sat next to her. Her head fell. He put his arm round her shoulders. She pulled herself away, turned to Jack, shaking.

"Father -" she began. "I've done a terrible thing -"

"Keep quiet!" Victor ordered, trying to force her away from Jack. "Leave this to me."

Jack sensed Ricky in the doorway, watching. He looked up. Ricky shook his head at him.

Victor began to speak: "I take responsibility for not protecting this family." Efigenia's chest was heaving. "The area of New Cebu was cleared last night."

"Ricky!" Jack shouted. "Quick!" The two young men ran to the door.

As they started the jeep, Victor, struggling with Efigenia, emerged from the house.

"Wait! Wait!" Efigenia was shouting. Unable to deter her, Victor helped her into the rear.

They moved steadily on the tarmac road.

"Faster!" Victor snapped.

"Should we say the Rosary?" Efigenia asked.

No one answered.

Coming up to Tagum, Jack slowed Ricky down.

"Not far now - "

"How is it you know the way?" Victor demanded.

"Look for a track on the left."

"How does he *know?*" Efigenia hissed.

"Leave him."

"There!"

Ricky swung the wheel: "Would have missed that -"

"You can't go far up but - "

Rounding a bend Ricky slammed on the brakes. "Whoa!"

"What in God's name – "

Victor jumped out: "Hand me an axe!"

Ricky pulled the axe from under the seat by the emergency spade. His father began hacking at a wooden barricade across the track with a ROAD CLOSED BY ORDER sign.

They drove on.

"Oh no - !"

To one side of the track stood Norma's car. It was not damaged. She was not inside.

"This is the last place she'd have counted on being able to turn - "

"How does he *know*?"

"Drive on!"

"Stop!"

Victor climbed out slamming the door on Efigenia.

"I will not have a woman come. You stay here. Fr Jack, keep her company. Ricky!"

They fell from sight.

"Pray, Father."

"I am praying."

Flies buzzed in and out. How could this be happening? To Norma?

"Oh Father!" Efigenia bleated. "They are so cruel!"

"Norma is resourceful – "

Walking ahead Victor found slashed and flattened bushes where vehicles had turned, tyre marks; boot treads narrowing on a tight path where branches scratched their heads.

"Wait!" Victor blocked the way. I don't want you to see this."

"Is it Norma?"

Pushing past him, Ricky saw a piece of string drawn across the path at chest height, studded at intervals with human ears, some very small. His father was sliding them like abacus beads, checking.

"Not Norma's." He ducked under them.

"Stop!" Ricky grabbed his arm, pointing to wires running into the leaf mould.

"That's bluff!" Victor bent, tugged the wires. Instantly they came free.

"Listen! Listen!" They could hear Efigenia hallooing. And shots.

Quickly they scuttled back. Efigenia was leaning against their vehicle, stoutly defending herself against two INP men.

"We are not trespassing!" she shouted. "We are retrieving my daughter's car!"

"Ah!" Victor advanced on them, arm outstretched. "I am Victor Salcedo."

"If you are collecting that car, why weren't you with it?"

"Looking for the steering nut," Ricky said calmly. "It fell off. That's why she abandoned it."

"So where is she?"

"At home of course waiting for her car!" Efigenia snapped. "Will you leave us?"

"Get into your vehicle. You are under escort to Tagum. Your daughter's vehicle will be towed."

"Most kind." Victor slipped him some notes. "Towards the tow truck."

"You knew about this place!" Efigenia hissed at Jack as they bumped ahead of the INP jeep into Tagum. "Make him get out Ricky!"

"Be quiet."

"There's another way in – "

"Where?" Ricky asked.

"I'll show you."

Dropping Efigenia and Victor on the bus route, they sped along the old trunk route.

"Next bend. *There!*"

Ricky slid into the siding Norma had discovered, climbed out and entered the darkening forest, its air thick with small things moving in the trees, humming, biting things. Without speaking they slashed their way up 'til they hit the grass track leading down to the East.

"How far is it?"

"Hurry."

Another thirty minutes took them to the ridge where below in the valley, a white mist hung over the lake, sucking towards itself wisps of smoke from the remains of charred houses. No sound. No voice. They descended. The half- light picked out a pink flip-flop, a blouse, a set of teeth…. guarded by still smouldering ruins…

"Nor - maaah!!" Ricky shouted. The sound reverberated.

They split up and searched. The moon rose.

Encountering each other at a corner, they were without words. They left the valley.

On the crest, they stood in the dark. Ricky began to weep. They turned from each other. Before Jack's eyes rose the image of the first church he had wandered into on that bus journey across Mindanao. The evaporated milk tins with paper flowers in them, the backdrop of painted rice fields on the peeling plaster wall, the confessional's yellow shower curtain - above the altar, the figure of Christ swaying gently in a breeze from the door. Hands and feet nailed. A good man, unable to move but for the turning of his head. Tossed by the currents around him. Ordinary peasants would have been there, watching, helpless, expecting it. The crucifixion of the good by the greedy.

"Do you think we'll find her?" Ricky asked.

"We might."

"Alive?"

"It's possible."

He stared into the dark hole where the valley lay.

"We'd better get back." Jack moved towards the forest, the difficulty of the descent in darkness allowing them time to retrieve control. What was the question he had asked himself in that church so long ago? And the answer that had come to him in Ah Chan's store?

Ricky began speaking.

"I can't remember my parents taking a public bus before – "

"Must've. When they were young."

Involuntarily Ricky slowed as they approached the house. Jack got out first. Ricky reversed and parked up. Jack waited. The front door was open and lights on inside. But no sound. Ricky entered first. Guinaldo was at the top of the stairs blocking them. He locked eyes with Ricky who hurried to the lounge, turned to beckon Jack. Victor, his back to them, hair awry, shirt pulled from his trousers, was doing something to Efigenia, her breathing hard, loud.

"Let me *go!*" She flung him off!

"Stop her!" Victor shouted, face bloody, blood on the walls and furniture. "She's self-harming!" Efigenia lunged for a large knife by his feet but Ricky kicked it away, grabbed her arm, already laced with slashes.

"Let – me – *do* – it!" she screamed. They forced her to the sofa. Victor burst into tears.

"Towels!" Ricky called.

Victor tried to stroke her head, pull her to him but she reared away, howling: "What have I done?!" Then turned to look at them. For a moment there was silence.

Ricky and Jack exchanged glances. Both knew where their futures lay.

It was time to begin.

Printed in Great Britain
by Amazon